Seeking Cassandra

Lutricia Clifton

Holiday House / New York

HOLIDAY HOUSE is registered in the U.S. Patent and Trademark Office.
Printed and Bound in March 2016 at Maple Press, York, PA, USA.
www.holidayhouse.com
First Edition
1 3 5 7 9 10 8 6 4 2

Library of Congress Cataloging-in-Publication Data
Names: Clifton, Lutricia, author.
Title: Seeking Cassandra / by Lutricia Clifton.
Description: First edition. | New York : Holiday House, [2016] |
Summary: Twelve-year-old Cassie discovers that first impressions can be misleading—and potentially damaging—when she leaves her ritzy neighborhood in Austin, Texas, to spend the summer with her divorced father in his Winnebago camp trailer in Palo Duro Canyon State Park.
Identifiers: LCCN 2015031260 | ISBN 9780823435609 (hardcover)
Subjects: LCSH: Palo Duro State Park (Tex.)—Juvenile fiction. | CYAC: Palo Duro State Park (Tex.)—Fiction. | Mystery and detective stories.
Classification: LCC PZ7.C622412 Se 2016 | DDC [Fic]—dc23 LC record available at http://lccn.loc.gov/2015031260

For my sons, Jeffrey and Christopher

ACKNOWLEDGMENTS

The setting of this book is genuine. Names, characters and incidents are fictional. Information from the *Junior Naturalist Program* is used courtesy of the Texas Parks and Wildlife Department, with my deepest appreciation.

Thanks also to my incredibly talented editors at Holiday House, Julie Amper and Kelly Loughman, for helping me tighten the seams and smooth out the wrinkles.

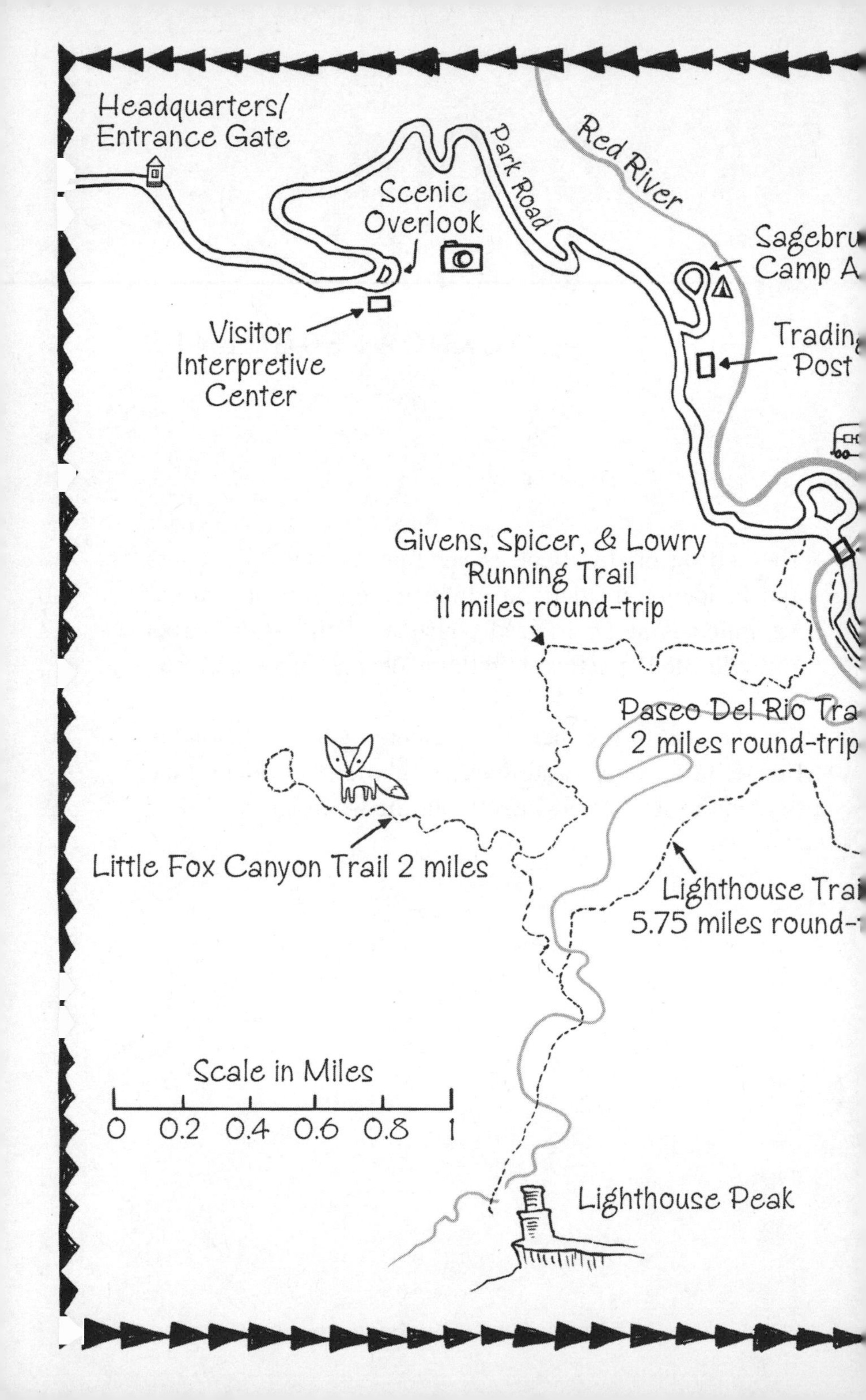

Headquarters/
Entrance Gate
Park Road
Red River
Scenic
Overlook
Visitor
Interpretive
Center
Trading
Post
Givens, Spicer, & Lowry
Running Trail
11 miles round-trip
2 miles round-trip
Little Fox Canyon Trail 2 miles
Scale in Miles
0 0.2 0.4 0.6 0.8 1
Lighthouse Peak

Hackberry Camp Area

Red River Flash Flood Point

Chinaberry Day Use Area

Red River Flash Flood Point

Rojo Grande Trail 2 miles

Sunflower Trail
2 miles round-trip

Juniper Trail—Riverside
2 miles round-trip

Mesquite
Camp Area

Dump
Station

Red River
Flash Flood
Point

Juniper Trail—Cliffside 6 miles round-trip

Red River Flash Flood Point

CHAPTER ONE

"Hey, Peaches! When did you get so big? Not too big to give your old man some sugar, I hope."

Sugar. My dad's word for a kiss.

Old man. His term for "father."

Peaches. His nickname for me.

"Dad, my name's Cassie."

"Actually," he says, "it's Cassandra, after a girl in Greek myth. . . ."

Oh, no—that old story that grosses me out.

"You remember . . . snakes licked Cassandra's ears so clean she could understand the language of animals—"

"I *know,* Dad. But call me Cassie. It's what *everyone* calls me."

His shoulders droop a little. "Cassie it is," he says.

His whiskers scratch when I kiss his cheek. "You grew a beard . . . your clothes . . . you moved here. *Why?*"

I had a window seat on the flight from Austin to Amarillo. When we circled to land, the ground below looked like a big brown pancake. I don't eat pancakes. They taste like Play-Doh unless you put a ton of butter and syrup on them. But butter and syrup are on Mom's *verboten* list. *Verboten* is German for "forbidden." In French, it's *tabou*. Mom's studying foreign languages.

"Why'd I move here? Why'd I grow a beard? Or . . ." He looks down at his clothes. "What's wrong with the way I'm dressed?"

"Why . . . *all* of it?"

I haven't seen Dad since Christmas, when he left Austin, but he calls me every weekend. He and Mom divorced two years ago when I was ten, and they share custody of me. I spent every other weekend with him before he moved. Back then, he shaved and cut his hair short. Wore shoes instead of lace-up boots with scuffed toes. A suit and tie, not faded jeans and a shirt with holes at the elbows. He looked nice then—handsome, even.

"Well . . ." His mouth smiles, but his eyes still look shipwrecked. "Your mom wanted to follow her dream, so I decided to do the same."

"*This* is your dream?" As far as I can see, the land is flat—clear to the horizon.

"Just wait," he says. "It gets better."

We walk to the parking lot, my big black suitcase bumping along after my dad, my day pack bumping against my shoulder blades. A bossy wind is blowing, kicking up dust that stings my eyes, twisting my hair into knots. Barely able to see, I crash into Dad when he stops.

I look around for his SUV, a red Mazda with gray leather seats, but Dad lifts my suitcase into the back end of a dirty blue pickup with a long metal box behind the cab.

"You drive a *truck*?"

"Yep. This Chevy suits my needs now. The CXT would tow a lot more weight, but it had a hefty price tag. . . ."

I tune Dad out as he talks about towing capacity, gas mileage and telescoping mirrors. A minute later, I tune him in again.

" . . . but the International cost more than this carpenter can afford, so I bought this one. It got good ratings, too."

"Carpenter?" The metal box in the back end suddenly makes sense. It's a toolbox. "Your dream was to become a *carpenter?*"

My dad used to work for a software company in Austin, like my mom still does. She's on her way to Europe to attend a six-week training course for managers. He was already a manager, working in technical support, but he quit his job when he moved away. And all the times we talked, he never said a word about any of this. Why? Has he totally flipped out?

He pauses, thinking. "More of a construction worker, I guess. I do painting jobs, too. Some plumbing, electrical. Little bit of everything." Rubbing the back of my head like he did when I was a little girl, he says, "Hop in. Don't want to ruin the surprise."

More surprises?

Yay, me.

CHAPTER TWO

The truck shakes like a blender crushing ice cubes, and sounds like one, too. I cling to the grab handle and look at Dad.

"Diesel runs a bit rougher than regular gas," he says. "It'll smooth out once we get going." As the truck changes from loud rumbling to low grumbling, he looks at me again. "That, uh, that wash out?"

He's looking at my hair, which is honey brown . . . mostly.

"It's called dip dying, and no, it doesn't wash out. That's why my friends and I only do the ends. It gets cut off when you trim it, but you can have it dyed again. Mandy and Beth do theirs a different color every time. Pink . . . blue . . . green—sometimes more than one."

"Mandy and Beth?"

"My best friends."

"You meet them at that private school your mom insisted on?"

Right before Christmas this year, Mom moved us

to a neighborhood on the other side of town. She said it was safer and the new school had better teachers and a college-prep curriculum. Gang violence was becoming a problem where we used to live, and gang members had started harassing kids at the public school I attended. You could always spot them, especially the ones who wore jackets with their gang name on it and had their gang's symbols tattooed on their necks or arms. In Texas, you have to be eighteen to get tattoos, but these kids obviously knew how to get around the law. Nobody had given me any trouble yet, but Mom seemed to think it was only a matter of time.

I really missed my friends after we moved. We talked a lot right at first, but not so much anymore. They got busy with clubs and cheer squad, and I had a lot of catching up to do at my new school.

"Cassie?" Dad was still waiting for me to answer his question.

"Yeah, I met them at school. They're real cool. We do everything together."

That isn't exactly true. It was only a few weeks ago that Mandy and Beth let me be their friend, and that was because we were assigned a group paper. I did most of the work, but I didn't care. After we turned in our paper, they asked me to go to the mall with them. *Me*, the bookworm at the back of the room. Right off, they decided I had to do my hair like theirs. I said no at first, but when they called me a wimp, I caved.

"And your mom is okay with it?"

"Well, sure . . ." I look out the window, watching a flat world rush past. "Totally."

That's not exactly true, either. Mom pitched a fit when

she saw my hair. But when I told her all the kids were doing it, she eased off. "A fad," she mumbled. "A passing fad." Her way of saying I was to get my hair back to normal as soon as possible.

But I really wish she'd liked it. . . .

I look at Dad. "Mandy and Beth love it—me, too. Do, uh, do *you* like it?"

"Didn't see anything wrong with the way it was," he says.

My chest caves in. "Well, I picked my favorite color. It's called—"

"Peach," he says, finishing for me.

"Oh, yeah."

When I was six, I asked Dad to paint my bedroom a peach color. He mixed and mixed until he got the shade exactly right.

"Becoming a construction worker isn't the dream I was talking about," he says, changing the subject.

"Then what is?"

"A picture's worth a thousand words," he says.

That's the big difference between my dad and my mom. She's a motormouth and he'd rather read words than speak them. Before he left Austin, he went to the library every weekend. I don't know why. He owned enough books to open a bookstore.

Sighing, I stare at lines in a highway that goes on for miles and miles.

"Guess it'll grow on me," he says a few minutes later.

"Thanks, Dad."

CHAPTER THREE

Ahead of us, I spy the outlines of tall buildings. A town. A *big* town. My stomach gets jumpy as I think about cool stores and water parks that I can tell Mandy and Beth about. They're stuck in Austin all summer doing the same old things.

I hope they won't be jealous. I hope they still like me when I get back. Maybe I'll get my hair double-dipped—even triple.

The turn signal on the truck begins to tick, a light on the dash blinks and Dad eases onto an asphalt road, taking us in a different direction.

"Wait—" I watch the town in the distance fade. "Where are we going?"

"Almost there."

Now the land outside the window isn't just flat, it's boring. Dry grass. Skinny cows. Sagebrush piling up along fences. Something in the distance gets my attention. I can't tell if it's real or a mirage, an optical illusion that happens in hot weather.

"Here we go." He turns onto a dirt track that leads to a pasture. "Hop out and open the gate—and close it behind you. Don't want the cattle getting out."

"*Yuck.*" I land in a plop of cow manure that stains my new pink Converses green. The manure swarms with black flies, which tag along after me. Swatting at them, I tug a rusty hinge free and drag a sagging gate across the road. After Dad drives through, I drag the gate shut again.

I'm covered in orange-colored dust and fly bites when I get back to the truck. Slamming the door, I look at Dad and say, "This dream better be good."

"It's better than good," he says, speeding up.

The mirage gets clearer, and a few minutes later, Dad stops in front of it: a paintless house practically buried under a drift of dry sagebrush.

"Here we are," he says.

"*This* is the surprise?" The wood siding on the house has faded to gray, the color of mildew. A metal roof sags in the middle. Other than spiky grass, sagebrush and knobby trees, there's not another thing in sight.

"No, this is where the original settler lived," Dad says. "The rancher who owns the property now built a new house. Nice guy. Gave me permission to come on his property."

"Dad, I don't want go in there." The house is spooky. Warped boards cover windows, and the roof is streaked with rust, like blood. "It's probably full of spiders and scorpions."

"Big ones, no doubt. Follow me and watch for rattlesnakes," he calls over his shoulder.

"Rattlesnakes?"

"Just listen to what they're telling you and you'll be

fine. If they rattle their tails, make a wide circle round them."

Eyes glued to the ground, I inch my way around clumps of yellowed grass, piles of sagebrush and stubby trees. Dad is so tall, he outdistances me easily. When I catch up with him, he pulls me to a stop, pointing at the ground ahead.

"Careful," he says. "Don't want to fall off the rim."

The ground at our feet drops away like a dirt waterfall. We're standing at the edge of a gorge. A *huge* gorge.

"It's called Palo Duro Canyon," he says.

"Palo . . . *what?*"

"Palo Duro," he repeats. "It literally means 'hard tree' in Spanish. Park rangers figure it probably refers to the mesquite trees that grow here. A fork of the Red River carved the canyon over thousands of years . . ."

For once, Dad's not word-shy. He tells how this is the second-biggest canyon in the continental United States, second only to the Grand Canyon. He says other things, too. About the battles that were fought here, the archaeological finds made and early pioneer places that have been preserved.

"Pretty, isn't it?" He looks at me, waiting for an answer.

"Yeah, *real* pretty." Late-afternoon light colors the canyon like a rainbow fallen to earth, changing the walls from turquoise at the top to pumpkin orange near the ground.

"That's called the Lighthouse." He points out a tall rock in front of us that looks like a mushroom. "It's over three hundred feet high from its pedestal to the top. The pedestal's that flat ledge there at its base."

"It's tall, all right."

"Length of a football field." He indicates a narrow

opening in the brush. "This animal trail leads down the canyon wall, but . . ." He points downward, toward the canyon floor. "See that trail? Only way to get to it that's open to the public."

Far below, a cleared trail ends near the foot of the rock mushroom.

"Hikers aren't supposed to leave the authorized trails," he goes on. "The rangers want to keep track of who enters the park." He looks at me. "It's against the rules to climb down from the rim. Okay?"

One thing I've noticed with grown-ups. Sometimes when they tell you things, they're really saying the opposite.

"You climbed down from the rim, didn't you, Dad? So you're you saying it's okay to break the rules sometimes?"

"Well . . ." His mouth shows the faintest hint of a smile.

I wonder if the daredevil next to me is really my dad. When he lived in Austin, he didn't do much of anything, except work and read books.

"But Dad, I don't get it. If seeing this was your dream, why didn't you just take off a couple of weeks from work? I mean, why'd you have to *move* here?"

"Because . . ." He sweeps the hair out of his eyes. "I didn't want to just see *this* place. I wanted to see other places, too. This work lets me do that."

"Why didn't you tell me? Why'd you keep it a secret?"

"I just thought it was best. You've had enough to adjust to lately. A new home, new school . . . and I needed to get my new business up and running." He turns to look at me. "And I was concerned that if I told you, you might not want to come." He indicates the country around us. "Let's face it. This is not what you're accustomed to."

"I see," I say, wishing I'd stayed with one of my grandparents, even though they live out in the country, miles from civilization. "Can we go now?" A cocoon of insects envelops me. "These bugs won't go away."

He leans close, sniffing. "What did you put on your hair?"

"Nothing. I mean, just shampoo and conditioner."

"Scented?"

"Mango peach. It smells real good."

"Yeah, well, the flies think so, too. We'll have to fix that. Come on, let's head back."

Fix what?

CHAPTER FOUR

The diesel engine rumbles to life and we leave the old house in a trail of swirling dust. Dodging cow plop and swatting flies, I open and close the sagging gate again and hurry back to the truck. As we bump along, I watch for the city on the horizon, thinking about a refreshing shower. A swimming pool. Air-conditioned movie theaters. Whenever Dad glances at his side mirror, I take a good look at him, but he doesn't seem to notice. A few minutes later, he pulls off at an entry gate with a sign that says PALO DURO CANYON and stops at a security hut.

"Need a map of the canyon, Fred," he says to a man inside.

In the lane opposite us at the exit gate, a large, square woman in a khaki shirt, green pants and Smokey the Bear hat is arguing with a man standing outside a dust-covered SUV.

"Open the back end," she tells him. Her hair is a burnt yellow and the skin on her cheeks is rough and red, like it's been rubbed with sandpaper.

"That's Winnie Burns," Dad says, his voice low. The uniformed woman sorts through things in the car. Backpacks, jackets, a cooler.

"What's she doing?"

"Winnie's a park ranger. She's in charge of the Naturalist Program, among other things. Not sure what's going on here."

The woman is still talking to the man when we drive away.

I look over my shoulder, watching her. "Gee, she's big and . . . and *square*. She could be a football player."

Dad laughs quietly. "Yeah, Winnie's more a burly girl than a girly girl, and she's one of the smartest people I ever met. Expert on wildlife and artifacts. Knows this canyon like the back of her hand."

"Can she do that . . . can she stop people like that?"

"She can if they're on park property." He glances at me. "Her bark's worse than her bite. You'll like her. She's a nice gal."

"Nice—? Dad, she was wearing a gun."

"Saw that." He blinks slowly. "Game wardens can carry weapons, and park rangers can serve in that capacity, too. Winnie keeps a close eye on the archaeological sites in the canyon, especially when it comes to making sure nothing's taken out. Sometimes tourists pick up souvenirs."

"Think she'll put that guy in jail?"

"Don't know." He hands me the map he picked up. "This is for you. It points out all the key sights and hiking trails. Canyon's a hundred twenty miles long, but this end's the only part open to the public." He glances at me again. "Thought you'd like to see where I work."

"Yeah, that would be cool."

I do want to see what Dad does now. He's worked with computers as long as I can remember. I can't imagine him working with a hammer and nails instead of cables and Wi-Fi.

I follow along on the map as Dad points out the Visitor Center, a trading post and several buildings he's repairing that were built by something called the Civilian Conservation Corps a long time ago. Driving farther, he points out rock formations, rest areas and trails and camping spots named after plants. Hackberry and Chinaberry. Sunflower and Juniper. After a while, things start to look the same.

"That outcropping's called the Sad Monkey." He points to a red sandstone formation. "See the face in the rocks?"

"Um . . ." I squint. "Um . . ."

"Well," he says, "the light needs to be just right, I guess."

As he drives deeper into the canyon, I start to squirm. Mom told me to look upon this trip as a fun adventure. So far, I've seen a deep canyon, parking places named after plants and piles of rocks that supposedly look like a lighthouse and a sad monkey. Interesting, but not my idea of fun or adventure.

Dad slows at a spot where the road goes through a small creek. The posted speed limit is five miles per hour. Shallow brown water swirls around the truck's wheels as he drives through it.

"These low-water crossings are given to flash flooding." He tilts his head toward the surrounding hills. "Canyon walls act like blinders, so a storm can be on top of you before you know it. It starts to rain, keep your eyes on the skies and steer clear of water crossings." He looks at me. "Got it?"

An uneasy feeling starts up in my stomach.

"Cassie?"

"I *heard* you, Dad. I'm not deaf, you know."

After fifteen slow miles and several low-water crossings, my stomach reminds me of something else. "I'm kind of tired and hungry. Can we go to your house now?"

"Figured you'd be hungry as a bear," he says. "Got supper all planned."

The turn signal ticks. The light on the dash blinks. Dad turns at a sign that says MESQUITE CAMP AREA. RV campers line a driveway, like a wagon train that's been circled against attack. I hold on to the roof handle as Dad bumps his way past the other campers and down a short dead-end road. He parks next to a camper with WINNEBAGO painted on its side.

"Home sweet home," he says.

The diesel engine stutters to silence. The city on the horizon disappears like a mirage. The queasy feeling in my stomach balloons.

Mom—I have to call Mom.

CHAPTER FIVE

"You live here?" I stare at the Winnebago camp trailer.

"Just until my work contract ends, then I'll move on." Dad lifts my suitcase, freckled now with pumpkin-colored dust, out of the truck. "Arrived ahead of the others, so I got my pick of places. I liked this spot because it's a bit more private. Can still see our neighbors, but they're not on top of us."

Private? The place looks like pictures of Mars on the Science Channel. Rocky red ledges and gnarled mesquite trees border the back of the camp spot. Cloud shadows creep up and down nearby canyons like dark ghosts.

"And you live in *that*?" I point at the Winnebago, a dusty metal box on wheels.

"Just like a turtle," he says, grinning at me, "I take my house with me."

Dad's camper is the kind that hitches to the back of his truck. Other types are parked around the campground. The kind you drive. The kind you pull. The flat kind that cranks up. A picnic table sits underneath a shade shelter beside each one. I can see fire rings next to the shelters, smoke rising from some. Looking at the one next to Dad's, I see a cooking grill balanced on the black, sooty rocks, flies buzzing above it.

No way, I think, almost gagging. *I'm not eating a morsel of food cooked on that thing. . . .*

"Some of the other people here at the Mesquite are longtimers, too." He knocks the dust off my suitcase with the flat of his hand. "Staying for more than a weekend."

The place hums with activity. Men stoking up fires in fire pits or pouring charcoal briquettes into grills they've brought along. Women hanging wet things on makeshift clotheslines, setting dishes on picnic tables. Kids walking to and from a cement block building in the middle of the campground, carrying beach towels.

Two boys leave the building and walk toward us. The shorter boy's wearing jean shorts and no shirt or shoes. The taller one has on cutoffs, flip-flops and a black tee with a logo on the chest: a skull and crossbones inside a three-sided warning sign, the word AGUAS! underneath.

"What's that mean, the word on that boy's shirt?"

Dad pauses to look. "Across the border, it would translate as 'Be careful' or 'Danger.' It's also a slogan that means something like 'Don't mess with me.' "

"So it's sort of a warning?"

"Sort of," he says.

I watch the boy as he nears. His hair is long and black, almost to his shoulders, and I can see long black lashes fringing dark eyes.

"What's up, guys?" Dad asks as they walk over.

"How you doing, Lucas?" A damp towel is slung over the taller boy's shoulder. He carries a cotton tote with clothes sticking out the top.

"We went swimming." The younger boy is missing two front teeth. He carries a damp towel, too. "And I trapped a fish with my hands."

"That's good, Héctor. Big enough to fry up for supper?"

"Yeah, but X didn't let me keep it."

"A minnow," X snickers. "It was a big minnow."

"You don't let me do anything," Héctor says, bottom lip jutting.

"Tell you what." Dad squats, eye level with the boy. "Next time you go fishing, use my rod and reel. It's in the locker on the other side of the camper. You know the one?"

Héctor nods, grinning.

"You, uh, you find them, Lucas?" X says. "I left them . . ." He uses his chin to point toward the Winnebago. "You know, the usual place."

"I did, X. I'll check them over tonight and we'll talk about it tomorrow."

"*Cool.* See you in the morning."

"Seven thirty," Dad tells him. "*Sharp.*"

X gives him a mock salute. As he walks past me, he says, "Welcome to the Mesquite, Cassandra." When he smiles, his teeth look snow-white next to his dark skin. Then something else catches my eye: tattoos have been permanently inked onto his arms. A bloody knife. Smoking gun. Grinning skull.

Just like the gangs at my old school did. . . .

"You smell good," Héctor says as he walks by.

"Um, thanks."

"Welcome," he says, grinning.

The boys walk toward one of the other campers and I turn to my father.

"Who are they? How'd they know my name? And . . ." I look toward the cement block building. "You have to shower *there*?"

"They're Roberto's boys. Told them you were spending a few weeks with me." He glances at the bathhouse. "Their camper doesn't have a shower. Mine does, but to keep from running short on water, I shower there, too."

I look at the two boys again. "Who's this Roberto guy? And what kind of name is X?"

"Roberto García works with me—and you're to call him Mr. García. I manage the carpentry work and he handles the masonry. He's a genius with concrete. I'd like him to work with me all the time, but don't know if he'll go for it. He wants to keep X in regular school for a while, and Héctor will start this year, too."

The boys stop at a camper half the size of the Winnebago. X pulls damp clothes out of the tote bag and hangs them over a rope strung between posts.

"And X is just a nickname," Dad says. "His full name is Xavier Rodriguez García." He looks at me, the hint of a smile showing. "Almost as bad as Cassandra, isn't it?"

"Yeah, *almost*."

Finishing with the clothes, X walks toward a gang of kids clumped in the shade of a scraggy mesquite. Héctor starts to follow, but X makes him go back.

I feel bad watching Héctor sitting alone on their front steps. Seeing him look our way, I wave at him. He waves back. Wondering why X wouldn't let Héctor go with him, I look toward the other kids, who look to be about eleven or twelve. A round boy and a blond girl sit on the sideline, watching three other boys in baggy jeans and T-shirts roughhouse with each other. Talking loud. Waving their arms around. Punching each other on the shoulder and chest. They're what my grandma would call toughs.

I bet they all have tattoos. . . .

When one of the boys spots me watching them, he laughs and says something to the other two. I feel my face turn warm as I hear more laughter, knowing he said something rude about me. As I start to turn away, I see X grab the boy by the shoulder and I hear him tell the boy to sit down or leave. In the afternoon light, X's face looks hard, menacing. It says *Don't mess with me. . . .*

I hold my breath, expecting a fight to break out, but it doesn't. Like someone turned off the TV, the laughing stops and the boys sit down.

Why'd they do that? Is X their leader?

CHAPTER SIX

"You like it?" Dad nods at the Winnebago. "Pulls like a dream. Good aerodynamics, smooth ride. Very little drag."

"Um, yeah. But it's kind of small."

Like a Dumpster on steroids, I think. No wonder Dad kept this new life a secret. He knew I'd hate it and would never have agreed to come.

"*Small?*" He eyes the camper again. "It's thirty-five feet long and equipped with everything you could need." He glances at me. "You don't like it?"

"No, it's great, Dad. Totally . . . great. . . ."

"Well, wait till you see the inside. Then we'll eat. Burgers are ready to throw on the grill. Turkey burgers, like your mom makes. And I picked up lots of fruit—apples, bananas, grapes—and whole-wheat pita bread. Your mom said you didn't eat anything but whole-wheat and multigrain breads and cereals."

My feet are glued to the ground. Stuck down with superglue.

He stares at me. "What is it, Cassie?"

"Dad, we have to call Mom. She wouldn't have let me come if she knew you lived here."

"Here?" He turns to look at the camper.

"And *here*." I wave my hand in the direction of the campground.

"I don't understand," he says, frowning. "I told your mom where I'm staying. And about the camper, my work . . ."

"You did?"

"You know we always discuss things that involve you, Cassie."

It's true. Other kids with divorced parents are always saying how their moms and dads argue and fight. Not mine. They talk about me all the time. My grades. My dentist appointments—even when I got my period.

"Except I told her to pack hiking clothes for you." He looks at my sequined tee and skinny jeans, the pink Converses. "Looser-fitting things. Heavy-duty."

"Hiking clothes? But these are the only kind of clothes I have. That *proves* it's all a mistake. Let's call Mom, *please?*"

"Cell phone reception's poor down here in the canyon," he says, frowning again. "Have to drive back to the entrance to reach a tower. Even then, the reception's not always good."

"E-mail, then. She checks her e-mail all the time."

"Same problem. Besides, your mom's boarded the plane for Munich by now. And when she lands, she'll be in a different time zone."

Oh, no, I think. That means I have to spend the night here. . . .

"Now, come on in," he says. "I invited the neighbors for supper. You need to meet them . . ."

. . . *and be polite.* He doesn't say the words, but I hear them loud and clear.

As I walk past the front window, something big and hairy and gray looks at me.

"A rat!" I shriek. "Dad, there's a rat in there."

"Not likely." Dad smiles, looking at the window. "That's Tiresias. Rat wouldn't stand a ghost of a chance with him around. Come on, I'll introduce you."

CHAPTER SEVEN

"See, the camper's not that small."

Dad sets my suitcase in front of a counter with a deep sink, cabinets above and below, and a microwave over a stove. A small refrigerator sits in the corner, with narrow pantry doors on either side.

"That extension makes it a lot bigger." He points his chin toward a long window seat, which sits farther back than the rest of the room. "That's your personal space. You'll sleep there, and the drawers underneath and cabinets overhead will provide plenty of room to stow your gear."

Is he kidding? I think, staring at him. There's no way I'm going to unpack. I'll be gone as soon as I talk to Mom.

"Compact, but comfortable," he says.

A recliner and TV fill up one end of the Winnebago, and a table and four chairs sit in the middle of the room. At the opposite end is a folding door, partitioning another room off from the rest. Behind it, I glimpse a full-sized bed. There's one other room with a door, right across from the entry. I peek inside. Small sink. Small toilet. And a small shower.

"Can I shower here tonight, not *out there*?" I thumb in the direction of the bathhouse.

"Okay, sure." He opens the folding door to the bedroom. "That's my space." A bookcase on one side of his bed is lined with books. A desk stacked with papers sits on the other side.

"And this is Tiresias." Dad picks up a charcoal-colored cat with ice-blue eyes. "Ti for short. Tiresias was a blind Greek prophet," he says, stroking the cat's head. "Supposedly a mystic."

"Mystic? You mean, like a magician?"

"More like a psychic. Someone who divines things, has special powers."

"*Right,*" I laugh. "Just like I can understand what animals are telling me. So you're saying the cat is blind?" I wave my hand in front of the cat's eyes. It doesn't flinch. "How does he get around if he can't see?"

"Relies on other senses. Every whisker's a sensor, even the hair on his body acts like radar. Hearing and smell are sharper, too. But you have to keep things picked up, else he'll get disoriented." He indicates two bowls on a rubber mat on the kitchen floor. One filled with water, the other with dry food. "That's his personal space." He points out two shelves on either side of the living room and one behind the TV. "Those window ledges, too. He follows the sunlight as it moves around the room."

"You're kidding, right?" I laugh again. Dad doesn't.

"Follows it like a sundial. Seems important to him."

Important to him? What about what's important to me?

"Why'd you adopt an old blind cat anyway?" I cross my arms, staring at the cat.

"Ti's not old. He was barely grown when I rescued him. Vet said some cat breeds are more prone to blindness than others. Had him almost six months now."

Six months. That's when he left Austin . . . and me.

"So the cat gets *four* spaces and I get one?" I stare at the window seat, my makeshift bed. At home, I have my own bedroom, *and* a bathroom with a tub.

"Five, if you count his litter box in the bathroom. I took the door off the bottom cabinet so it's always accessible."

I glare at the cat, my arms knotted across my belly.

"Look, Cassie," Dad says, sighing. "You can come and go as you please, do anything you want. But this is Ti's universe. He can never go outside. It wouldn't be safe."

I raise my hands palms up, open my eyes wide. "But it's not safe for me, either. Didn't you see that gang out there? Those tattoos X has on his arms?"

Dad's shoulders drop slightly. "It's what kids do where he lived. X is a good kid, the others, too. They'll be good friends."

"I already have friends—in Austin." I cross my arms again.

He sighs again, looking tired. "The way we lived in Austin isn't the real world, Cassie. Only about ten percent of the population lives that kind of life. It's like living in a . . . a cocoon." He nods toward the door. "*That's* the real world out there."

"Well, I like my world. There's lots of stuff to do there. Malls and movies and . . . stuff."

"Stuff." He shakes his head. "That's exactly what I'm talking about. Because of all the 'stuff,' you can lose sight of who you really are."

"I know who I am." I toss my hands in the air. "Besides, what am I supposed to do while you're at work?"

"Don't worry, I lined up some other activities for you. Which reminds me, your mom said she was sending something for you to do that's kind of related."

I remember the package in my day pack.

"Oh, *that*. It's just a book. She wrapped it up, but I can tell it's just a book."

"Let's take a look."

The package looks like it's been gift-wrapped for a six-year-old. Colorful balloons on the wrapping paper. A pink bow on the top. Mashed flat.

"Books are good things." Setting Ti on the window ledge behind us, Dad sits down next to me. "Open it up. Let's see what she sent."

I take off the bow, lift the tape on the back and remove the paper. It *is* a book, a book with blank pages.

"Why would she give me something like *this*?" I flip through the pages.

"Read the card," Dad says.

Cassie,

This is for keeping track of your adventures this summer. When I get back home, you can share them with me.

Love,

Mom

"Nice." Dad takes the book from me, examining it closely. "Real leather, brushed suede. Must've cost a pretty

penny." He smiles at me. "It's a good gift, Cassie, the perfect gift." He hands it back to me.

"It's a diary, Dad. She gave me a little girl's diary."

"No, it's a journal. Look at the inside page."

The front page says *This journal belongs to* . . . A blank line follows, with *Name* printed underneath.

"Same thing!"

"Not really. A diary's to write down what happens during the day. A record of sorts, like a newspaper. But a journal's for recording feelings, about what you did or what happened to you. Like a . . . a GPS that guides you. Sort of an internal navigation device."

"Dad . . ." I roll my eyes at him. "That is so *dumb*." I toss the journal on the window ledge. "I'm not going to write anything in that . . . *whatever* you want to call it, so what other activities have you lined up for me?" I stare at him, waiting.

He pauses, his eyebrows bunching. "No, you'll find out tomorrow. I think you need to spend some time tonight thinking about things." Looking at the window ledge, he says, "Anyway, looks like Ti's found a use for the journal."

I see the cat sharpening its claws on the journal's cover.

"Hey—" As I jerk the book away, the cat lashes out at me. "*Ow*—he tried to claw me."

Dad shakes his head slowly. "It's because you scared him. Remember, he's blind. Only natural that he'd try to protect himself. And the people who owned him before had his front paws declawed, so he can't actually hurt you *or* the journal. Take a look. You see any scratches?"

No scratch marks on my arm. I examine the cover of the journal. No scratches there, either.

"Well, you said it cost a lot of money. He'll get cat hair all over it."

"Cassie . . ."

"Okay, okay. But if Mom gets mad 'cause it's covered in cat hair and spit, you have to explain."

"Deal," he says. "Now, the Stovalls will be over any minute. Wash up, we're eating outside. You can unpack later."

I toss the journal back on the shelf. Immediately, Ti lies down on it and goes to sleep. Sighing, I join Dad in the kitchen. He takes burger patties and hamburger buns, baked beans and potato salad in plastic tubs from the refrigerator. Most of the food is on Mom's *verboten* list, but my stomach is growling like a bear and I'm actually really looking forward to chowing down.

"Oh . . ." Dad pauses at the door. "Bring that spinach salad when you come. Your mom said to make sure you got plenty of dark, leafy greens. I fixed that especially for you."

Yay, me.

CHAPTER EIGHT

"Well, now. Aren't you a pretty little thing."

Mrs. Stovall—she insists I call her Pearl—has blue eyes and a big smile. Her blunt-cut gray hair is lopsided, a sign she's her own barber. She's wearing knee-length shorts, a man's plaid shirt and roll-top socks stuffed in ankle-high walking boots. Her husband—I'm supposed to call him Charlie—is dressed pretty much the same except he wears suspenders to keep his shorts from falling down. His white hair looks home-cut, too, but shorter. When Dad introduced them, he said they were the campground hosts. They live in the camper closest to his. Their little white poodle is named Okie-Dokie and wears a red bandana around his neck.

"Interestin' hair," Charlie says, studying the back of my head. "Must've inherited it from your mom. Funny, idn't it, the genes we get stuck with?"

Dad hides a grin. I roll my eyes at him.

Charlie supervises my dad, who scrubbed the grill

with a wire brush before grilling the burgers. While I set the table, Pearl puts out other foods. She brought a picnic basket stocked with all kinds of things.

Pearl and Charlie do the talking during supper. Mostly about people who have come in or will be leaving. I don't pay much attention. I'm more interested in what's happening at a campfire across the way, the one where X and the other kids hang out. Firelight flickers across their faces, but I can't hear what they're saying. Just the sound of soda cans popping, and giggling. I wonder if they're still talking about me.

"We shoveled that down pretty good, didn't we," Charlie says as Pearl brings out dessert. A Dutch-oven peach cobbler, cooked on their fire pit, with whipped cream in a can for topping.

"I could've eaten a steer walking," Dad says. "Fresh air sure gives you an appetite."

"More cobbler, Cassie?" Pearl says.

"Maybe a little."

She fills my bowl to the top.

"What about the spinach salad?" Dad looks at the uneaten salad on my plate. "You hardly touched it."

"She's a growing girl, Lucas," Charlie says. "Needs stick-to-the-ribs food, not rabbit fodder."

I feel a little guilty, thinking of Mom. Then I think how it's only for one night and squirt more whipped cream on my second helping of dessert.

As Dad and the Stovalls start talking again, I look around the Mesquite. Fire pits and lanterns glow like giant fireflies. Smoke hangs over the ground like a mist, smelling of mesquite wood and charcoal. Stars come out above canyon walls that are now pitch-black. Suddenly an eerie howling echoes across the canyon, and dogs at other campsites start to bark.

I look at Dad. "What was *that*?"

"Nothing to worry about. Just coyotes after small game."

"Dogs and cats, too." Pearl calls Okie-Dokie, who's been exploring the rock ledges around the campsite, and ties his leash to a post.

"Before we turn in," Charlie says, "we'll walk around and tell newcomers to keep their pets inside. Those yappy things have been on the prowl a lot lately. Don't know what's got 'em so upset." He looks at Dad. "You hear about the pilfering?"

"Catch me up." Dad pours Charlie another cup of coffee. "Saw Winnie searching a car when we came in."

Winnie. The burly park ranger who carries a gun . . .

"Don't know much. Guess artifacts at one of the Indian dig sites disappeared. Sure got Winnie on the warpath."

"Where'd you hear that?" Dad asks.

"Came in over the two-way," Pearl says.

"What's a two-way?" I ask.

"Radio," she tells me. "Cell phone reception's rotten down here in the gulch. To communicate with headquarters, we use a two-way radio. We're only supposed to use it in an emergency, though."

"Catch who did it?" Dad asks.

"Not yet," Charlie says. "Winnie's been searchin' cars at the front gate all day. They must've left the canyon before the theft was discovered."

"All kinds of ways to get in and out of this canyon besides the front gate," Dad says.

Charlie raises shaggy white eyebrows. "You think they came and went from the rim?"

Dad shrugs.

"Maybe they didn't leave yet." I glance toward the shadowy figures across the campground, thinking how gangs break the law. Vandalism. Robbery. Looking for X, I see him feeding wood to the fire, sending sparks shooting into the air like sparklers.

"Well, now," Charlie says, nodding slowly. "There's an interestin' thought."

"Lord help, let's get this table cleared." Pearl scratches her arms. "Bugs are 'bout to carry me away. Don't know why they're so bad tonight."

Dad looks at me.

I feel my face redden, heat rising in my cheeks.

"Might be a sign of rain," Charlie says, looking at the sky. "Insects and animals can predict the weather, you know."

"It is time to wrap this up," Dad says, looking my way. "I have paperwork to catch up on and Cassie needs to unpack—and shower before she goes to bed."

Now my face blazes.

"You need anything while you're here, honey," Pearl says, giving me a bear hug, "we're right close. Come over anytime, I'll show you how to cook over a campfire."

"Thanks," I wheeze through squeezed lungs. I feel deceitful, not telling her I'll be leaving tomorrow.

The darkness outside the campground is the blackest black I've ever seen. No streetlights. No porch lights. No . . . anything. Except millions of stars. I want to stay outside to look at them, but the bugs won't leave me alone.

Back inside, Dad washes the dishes and I dry.

“I don’t want you going hiking alone, Cassie,” he says, peering through the window over the sink.

If he’s thinking about the pilfered sites, he has nothing to worry about. A gang of thieves operating in the canyon is just the fuel I need for an airplane ticket back to Austin. I catch my breath as another thought hits me.

Mom is bound to send me to a ticket to stay with her parents—or maybe one of her friends in Austin. Austin would be great because then I could still see Mandy and Beth. But anywhere she says is okay with me. As long as it’s not here.

“Set your suitcase on the front step when it’s empty,” Dad says after we’ve cleaned up. “I’ll store it tomorrow.” He walks toward his bedroom. “TV works most of the time. It doesn’t, there are plenty of books.” He looks at me, the hint of a smile showing. “Some of them even have words in them.”

“Read?” I moan. “That’s all I’ve been doing!”

“Lights out at ten. Need to be ready to leave by seven thirty sharp.”

That’s just what he told X. . . .

“*Good,*” I call out as his bedroom door closes. “That means we can call Mom *early.*”

“And if you don’t want to be bug bait tomorrow,” he calls through the folding door, “use my shampoo and skip the conditioner.”

The TV screen is a white blizzard and crackles with static. I unzip my suitcase to get out my pajamas and toothbrush, which I packed last so they’d be on top.

“Wha—*what?* Where did this stuff come from?”

My bag is stuffed with khaki walking shorts, camp

shirts and a waterproof Windbreaker. Ankle-high hiking boots and thick socks are jammed into one corner. A floppy hiker's hat into another.

Tears show up out of nowhere.

Spotting the journal, which Ti is lying on, I jerk it from under him and turn to the first page, which says, *This journal belongs to . . .*

CASSIE'S JOURNAL

Mom,

How could you do this to me? We moved clear across town so we'd be safer and then you send me to a place where wild animals eat cats and dogs, rattlesnakes hide in the grass, people steal things, and a scary park ranger searches people and their cars. There's even a gang of toughs living right in the same campground—and the leader is covered with tattoos! I'm afraid to go outside!

Some adventure this is! I hate it here. Hate it, hate it, hate it . . .

CHAPTER NINE

"Cassie—get up. Alarm went off five minutes ago."

"But Dad, that cat walked on my head—and he howled all night." I force myself to sit up, then fall back on the bed. My head thumping. My eyes dry and crusty from crying.

"I told you to keep things picked up—*and* to unpack your suitcase and set it outside. Ti got disoriented. When that happens, he gets scared." Dad glances at the mass of twisted bedcovers. "And make your bed. Or do you want Ti to get so confused he forgets where his litter box is?"

"Oh, geez, he wouldn't do that . . . would he?" I look for Ti as I pull the covers straight. He's lying on the shelf that gets the morning light, sleeping. "So that howling's his way of crying?"

"Pretty much."

"I didn't know," I mumble, feeling bad.

Dad dumps my clothes into one of the drawers under the bed and sets my suitcase on the front stoop. The heap of hiking clothes makes tears well up again.

"What's wrong now?" Dad asks, eyeing me.

"Sorry, Dad. I . . . I was sick last night."

"*Sick?* Well, you look all right to me. Besides, I'm not the one you owe an apology."

"Who . . . ?" His eyes travel to where the cat is lying. "The cat? You want me to apologize to a cat?"

"Let him sniff your hand, then rub his ears. He likes that."

I can't believe Dad is serious, but the stare he gives me says he is.

Reaching my hand out, I hold it in front of Ti. His nose feels cool to my fingers, velvety soft. Feeling stupid, I mumble, "Sorry."

Ti purrs loudly.

"Hey . . ." I run my hand over his head. "Does that mean something?"

"Means he likes it when you're nice to him. Now, get a move on. I have to drop you off at the ranger station at eight."

"Ranger station? Why?"

"Told you. I've lined up activities." He looks at me, eyes serious. "And another thing. This nonsense about calling Becky has to stop. She's *not* going to send you back to Austin."

"Yeah, I figured that out."

I hardly slept, thinking of Mom. So busy doing *her* thing, she forgot to tell me she was shipping me off to Nowheresville.

I look at Dad. "And so you know, she hates it when someone calls her Becky. She wants to be called Rebecca now. She said Becky sounds too . . . childish."

"*Childish?*" Mouth pinched, Dad sets milk and cereal

on the table and slips whole-wheat bread into the toaster. "We're leaving in fifteen, Cassie. Get dressed, you need to eat something."

I carry khaki shorts and a pink polo to the bathroom and dress. My hair looks like a brush pile because I didn't use conditioner when I shampooed last night. Pulling it into a ponytail, I return to the kitchen, where Dad's making a peanut butter and jelly sandwich.

"Is that for me?"

"Yep, don't have to worry about PB&J going bad in the heat." He slips the sandwich into a brown paper bag.

I pick up my Converses and sit down at the table.

"Not those," he says. "Wear the socks and boots your mom sent."

I grab bulky hiking socks and tug them on. "What will I be doing?" The boots are stiff, unbending.

"Don't worry," he says, smiling. "It's something fun."

Great. *More* surprises.

"Now, hurry up. We have to pick up four others."

My back stiffens. "Who?"

"Some friends."

"*My* friends are back in Austin—and I wish I was with them right now."

"Nothing in the rule book says you can't make new ones," he says.

CHAPTER TEN

X and Héctor are waiting outside the Winnebago, wearing faded shorts and T-shirts and scuffed hiking boots. Each carries a brown paper bag. Héctor also carries a tote.

"You don't mean . . ." I give Dad a look. "*No way.*"

"*Way,*" he says, eyes hard.

Two of the new friends have been identified.

"Dad," I say, squirming. "I don't mind staying here—*really*. Ti prob'ly gets lonely. . . ."

"Back end, Cassie." He gestures with his chin toward the truck. "I need to talk to X."

"But—"

"No arguing."

Stomping to the back of the truck, I watch X lower the tailgate and lift Héctor into the back end.

"Remember, no hanging off the side," X tells him. "If Lucas catches you, he won't let you ride with us." He holds out a hand to help me in.

"I don't need your help." Turning my back to him, I

hoist myself into the truck and plop down by the toolbox, knees hugged tight to my chest.

X walks away, eyebrows knit together.

"Hi, Cassandra." Smiling, Héctor sits down next to me, brown bag and tote clutched to his chest.

Still smoldering, I snap, "Don't call me that."

His smile disappears and his chin drops toward his lap.

Sighing, I nudge him on the shoulder. "Call me Cassie. I don't like Cassandra. Okay?"

"'Kay," he says, grinning.

A short man walks up to the truck. A faded red ball cap covers dark hair streaked with white. A matching mustache covers his upper lip.

"Welcome to the Mesquite, Miss Cassandra," he says, removing his hat.

"Thanks"—I glance toward Dad, who's watching with eagle eyes, listening with bat ears—"Mr. García."

"You do what Lucas tells you," Mr. García tells Héctor. "Study your books."

Héctor looks at me. "Lucas is helping me read."

"Oh?" The tote must be a book bag.

"But I get to eat lunch with you." He holds up his lunch bag.

"Yeah? That's great."

Mr. García turns to Dad. "Want me to start on that other building this morning?"

Dad nods. "Be there soon as I drop off the kids."

I watch Mr. García drive off in a red truck as faded as his hat, wondering why Dad wanted X to sit up front with him. What he needed to talk to him about. Why he couldn't talk to him in front of me. I lean as close to the rear glass as I can get, but all I can hear is a diesel engine, grumbling loud.

We stop near the entrance to the Mesquite to pick up a chubby boy and a slight girl wearing khaki shorts and T-shirts, with well-worn hiking boots. Both carry brown bags. Neither has tattoos. I recognize them from the campfire where X's gang hangs out.

New friends three and four.

Lowering the tailgate, the boy locks his fingers, making a step for the girl. She gives me the once-over as she sits down, her mouth a thin pencil line. Looking over the side of the truck, she stares into the distance, saying nothing. The boy is sweating by the time he closes the tailgate and hoists himself over.

"Hey, Cassandra," he grunts. "I'm Bobby Ray." He glances at the girl. "She's Glinda. You know, like the Good Witch in the *Oz* movie?"

Bobby Ray has light hair, gray eyes and three chins. His mouth is small and bowed, like Cupid. No taller than Héctor, Glinda has choppy blond hair, dry as corn husks, that frames an older-looking face.

"She wants to be called Cassie," Héctor says. "She don't like Cassandra. Her mom's in Europe."

My shoulders sag. I wonder if there's anything Dad *hasn't* told them.

"Oh, okay." Bobby Ray settles in next to the girl, cradling an oversized brown bag.

The diesel engine rumbles to life again. Leaving the Mesquite behind, we start the slow trip to the ranger station at the park entrance.

"So, Cassie," Bobby Ray says, talking over the engine. "You're here for the summer, huh?"

"Six weeks," I sigh.

"I'll be here all summer again. We came last year, too. My dad's doing research at the college. It's that way." He thumbs over his shoulder. "He's a botanist. Studies plants. My mom . . . well, she's just hangin' out. Her job's kind of stressful so she's resting up. They really like it here."

Glinda is as still as a stone, staring at the canyon walls as they slip past.

"Oh—" Bobby Ray notices I'm looking at Glinda. "Her folks teach at the college. I forget what. . . ." He looks at Glinda for help, gets none. "Teachers," he says, looking at me again. "They're teachers, but they park their camper at the Mesquite in the summer so they can hike."

"English and history," Glinda mumbles, not breaking her stare off the side of the truck. "English lit and American history."

Teachers and a scientist's kids? I glance at Bobby Ray and Glinda again. They don't look so tough anymore.

As the truck creeps along twisting roads and slogs through low-water crossings, I steal glances at Glinda, trying to figure out how old she is. Why she's so short.

Catching me staring, she rolls her eyes. "I was a preemie," she mutters.

"Preemie . . . ?"

"Born six weeks early. Stunted my growth. Weighed four pounds, two ounces." Picking up Bobby Ray's lunch bag, she tosses it to me like a football.

"Hey—you'll squash my chips," he yelps.

"*Wow.*" I catch the bag. Big for a lunch. Small for a

human baby. "That's pretty little." I toss the bag back to her. Bobby Ray intercepts it before she can.

"Barely sixteen inches long." She uses her hands as a measure.

"That's short, all right." Something tells me I'm not the only one Glinda has caught staring.

"Yeah. Don't figure I'm going to get much bigger than this." She plops a hand on top of her head, like it's a boulder holding her down. "Four foot six, seventy-two pounds. Soaking wet."

"Well, maybe you'll grow some more," I say, feeling the need to say something.

"Nope." She shakes her head. "Oh, there's a formula that factors in your mom and dad's heights, but the fact is, girls reach their maximum growth spurt at eleven or twelve. You know, when we go through puberty." She looks at me. "You get yours yet?"

"*Huh?*" I grunt, not believing she just asked me that. We don't even know each other!

I glance at Héctor, wondering if I should cover his ears. Sex education's not taught at my school until fifth grade, and I figure he's in kindergarten or first. But he's on his knees looking through the back glass. Watching X and Dad. Ignoring us.

Bobby Ray, however, *is* listening. His eyeballs bounce between Glinda and me like Ping-Pong balls. Boys act so dumb when it comes to girl things.

Glinda stares at me, waiting.

"Uh, yeah," I murmur, feeling my neck turn warm. "Couple months ago."

"Well, now . . ." Face and ears cherry red. Bobby Ray

swallows hard, like a wad of bubble gum is stuck to his tonsils. “How ’bout them apples?”

Glinda rolls her eyes at him, then looks at me. “Me, too. This is my view of the world.” She returns to staring off the side of the truck.

I look into the distance, too, watching canyon walls slip past. At five foot five, my view of the world is almost a foot higher than Glinda’s.

Still . . .

I look at her. “So you’re saying this is pretty much it for us?”

“Pretty much.”

Before my eyes, the canyon walls get taller.

CHAPTER ELEVEN

Dad pulls into the parking lot at a building marked PARK HEADQUARTERS. Ranger Winnie is waiting at the curb. Feet spread. Hands behind her back. Eyes barely showing beneath her Smokey the Bear hat.

"Morning, Winnie," Dad calls out. "Here are your new recruits."

"Thanks, Lucas. Pick 'em up 'bout four."

"Have fun, kids," Dad says as X, Glinda and Bobby Ray jump out of the truck. Héctor climbs out of the back end and crawls into the front seat. "Héctor will be back to eat lunch with you."

"*Fun?*" I whisper, walking past his door.

Smiling, he tosses me the floppy hiking hat Mom packed.

I watch him drive away, a hollow feeling in my stomach.

"*Cassandra!*" Ranger Winnie yells from the front door. "Get your butt in here. You're holding up the works." She gives me an up-and-down look as I walk inside, her eyes stopping at the pony logo on my pink polo shirt. "What do you think this is, girl? An amusement park?"

"No, ma'am," I mumble, hustling after Glinda, Bobby Ray and X.

It's a prison, I think. And the warden's name is Winnie.

"Take a seat," Ranger Winnie says, leading us to a room with a long table. "You'll sit in the same place this afternoon. No moving around."

I sit on one end, X on the other. Glinda and Bobby Ray fill in the middle chairs.

Ranger Winnie stands in front of us, still wearing her hat, still clutching her hands behind her back. She tells us we've been enrolled in the Junior Naturalist Program as guides to help summer students.

"I set up this junior guide position as an experiment because I'm swamped this summer. Don't know if I'll continue with it or not, it all depends on you. That means you're going to be in my spotlight, so don't screw up."

"Experiment," Bobby Ray whispers. "Oh, geez. Frankenstein was an experiment."

"Héctor's not old enough," Ranger Burns continues, "but because he can't stay alone, I've agreed he can hike with you once you finish the training. Understand?"

She makes eye contact with each of us. That looks says we're supposed to do something. We look at each other, then back at her.

"You're supposed to acknowledge you understand the terms and conditions," she says with a sigh.

X and Bobby Ray mumble, "Okay." Glinda mutters, "Why not." I hunch my shoulders and nod at Ranger Burns.

She rubs her face with both hands, looks at us again. "You're to call me Ranger Burns. Grown-ups can call me Winnie, but for you, it's Ranger Burns. Kids aren't taught to respect their elders these days. That's one of the things you'll learn working for me. Respect for people and the natural world. Now, raise your hand if you have questions."

No one raises a hand.

"Ask anything you want," she says. "You've got to be curious about something."

"Uh, okay." I inch my hand upward. "Why were you searching cars leaving the park yesterday?"

"What have you heard?" she asks.

"Something was stolen," Bobby Ray says.

The dagger and skull tattooed on X's arms draw my eyes like magnets.

"Artifacts," Glinda says. "My parents heard it was prehistoric artifacts."

Ranger Burns nods. "Plano points and a spearhead. *Plano* refers to a group of hunter-gatherers that lived here about five thousand years ago. The points are different from a lot of others you see in that they're not fluted." She looks around the table. "You know what that means? Fluted?"

Silence.

"Means these points haven't been hollowed out. They disappeared from a dig site that someone either knew about or stumbled onto. Archaeologist at the dig took a short lunch break and discovered them missing when she got back. Reported it right away, and that's when I started searching everyone going out—thoroughly. Little buggers are small, can be hidden easily."

I raise my hand again. "So points are just arrowheads? But I don't get it. Lots of people have collections of arrowheads. Museums, even."

"That's right, they do. But even *moving* an artifact is a federal offense in a state or national park. You see one—which you shouldn't if you stay on the trail—let it lie. Sometimes wind will uncover one. You do find one, mark it on your map and report it to me. And caution people against picking one up should they happen upon one."

She looks around. "Anything else?"

X's hand crawls into the air. "What're you going to do if you catch them?"

"Same thing that's done to any criminal."

"Pretty serious, huh?" he says.

"As a heart attack."

She looks around again. "Get your questions out of the way now. I'm pretty good at reading faces, so I know you have more."

Bobby Ray's hand inches up. "What if somebody needs to go potty and there's not a bathroom close?"

"Go potty . . ." Ranger Burns shakes her head, looking tired. "If you're talking number two, Bobby Ray, then you find a big bush, dig a hole and bury it. It would be a good idea to carry some TP and a digging tool in your backpack. Hand trowel . . . collapsible shovel. Just make sure you don't sit down on a rattlesnake or an ant bed."

Rattlesnakes? Ant beds? The hairs rise on the back of my neck.

Ranger Burns looks around again. Waiting.

I raise my hand once more. "Why us? I mean, why'd you pick us?"

"Now, *that's* a good question. You got tagged because

you're longtimers, not short-timers . . . and because I know your folks. What you'll be doing is fun, but serious. I need people I can rely on."

"So we'll be teachers for other kids that enroll in the program?" X says.

"That's right. Which means, you need to know the park inside out and upside down. You'll start a week from today, next Monday. That gives you plenty of time to complete the activity guide training and learn your trails."

"We got a head start," X says. "Héctor and I already hiked some of the trails."

"I've been hiking them for six years," Glinda says, sounding bored.

Six years? I look at Glinda, dumbfounded that she's been hiking since she was something like six.

"That's good, Glinda," Ranger Burns says. "But you need to know names and locations of *everything* in the park, not just the hiking trails. People will ask you all sorts of things, some of them pretty dumb. Doesn't matter, we treat every question with respect." She pauses. "Any of you want to bail out, now's the time to do it."

She looks around the table, lingering when she reaches me.

I want to run from the room, but there's no place to go.

"All right," she says, nodding. "Here, Cassandra, hand out these activity guides so I can see how much you already know. That'll give us a starting place."

CHAPTER TWELVE

A test. My first day of "fun" starts with a test. As junior guides, we'll help kids who enter the program learn all about the flora and fauna in the park and complete a list of activities, including hiking the trails. I can't even answer the first question, which is to name three animals that live in Palo Duro Canyon. The others rattle off animals like raccoons, opossums, squirrels, skunks, coyotes, deer and bobcats. Ranger Burns tells us there are even endangered species there, a mouse called the Palo Duro mouse and a lizard called the Texas horned lizard.

I raise my hand. "Those bobcats, aren't they dangerous? Don't they, you know, kill people?"

"Lions and tigers and bears . . . ," Glinda whispers. "*Oh, my.*"

Ignoring her, Ranger Burns looks at me. "You're probably thinking of mountain lions, Cassandra. Bobcats are a lot smaller. It's rare you'll see one. Wildlife in general avoids people." The corners of her mouth turn up a little. "Don't worry, you won't be doing anything dangerous.

Now, back to business. Everyone look at the study guide again."

Hearing someone whisper, "*Teacher's pet,*" I look to see which one it was, but they're all staring at me like I've come down with a tropical disease. Ignoring them, I look at the next part, which is to locate and name the four geologic layers in Palo Duro Canyon.

Geologic layers?

I raise my hand again. "This is hard stuff. Do we *have* to know it?"

"You'll be required to learn and remember this—and a lot more," says Ranger Burns.

As a throbbing starts up behind my eyelids, I read the next paragraph. We're to hike one of the trails and name four interesting things we see.

"Um," I say, easing my hand skyward. "How many trails are there?"

"A lot," Glinda says. "I know 'cause we come every year. The Givens Trail is eleven miles long, round-trip. The Lighthouse Trail is long, too, and has lots of offshoots. The Juniper-Cliffside's six miles. The Rylander Fortress Cliff Trail's a steep climb . . ."

My eyes glaze over as I listen to Glinda list all the trails in the canyon, plus the offshoots.

"Real good, Glinda," Ranger Burns says. "I plan to assign you to different trails, based on abilities and expertise, so your experience will be helpful."

Even though I'm sitting down, the muscles in my legs start to cramp.

Next, Ranger Burns asks us to name the river that runs through the park.

"I know this one," Bobby Ray says, waving a hand in the air. "It's the Red River. Right?"

"Specifically, the Prairie Dog Town Fork of the Red," Ranger Burns says. "Water erosion over millennia shaped the canyon and its formations. Water can be a powerful source in nature."

A thimbleful, I think. Somewhere I heard that a person could drown in a thimbleful of water. . . .

I groan as I read the next paragraph.

> Harvester ants (red ants) live underground in circular-shaped beds that are found throughout the park. They are the main food of a small, threatened lizard. For this reason, we do not destroy their homes. What is the name of this lizard?

"Probably that horned lizard you told us about," Bobby Ray says.

"Texas horned lizard," Ranger Burns says. "When you refer to it, use its correct name."

I raise my hand again. "Don't lizards bite?"

The others stare at me.

I shrug and say, "I heard they're poisonous so you shouldn't touch one."

"You never played with a lizard?" Glinda's eyes go round.

"Me? *No—*"

Ranger Burns rubs her head like it's throbbing. "Well, a bite from anything would hurt. Some worse than others, depending on what bites you. And a red ant bite would probably hurt worse, so watch out for them. Texas horned lizards can make themselves look scary, but it's just a defensive behavior."

"Scary . . . like how?"

"They puff up," X says. "Get real fat."

"Right," Ranger Burns says. "That's so they'll be hard to swallow. And when threatened, they sometimes squirt blood from their eyes, which tastes bad to certain predators. Mostly a scare tactic. Just keep in mind that these particular lizards are on the endangered list"—she glances at Glinda—"so *no one* should be picking one up."

Ranger Burns turns to me, the trace of a smile showing again. "But if you're ever inclined, Cassandra, pick one up behind its horns." She holds her thumb and forefinger like they're tweezers. "That way it can't squirt at you."

Like I'm going to pick up anything that has horns and squirts blood from its eyes!

"Who can tell me where the two historical markers are in the park and why they're there?" Ranger Burns asks.

Of course, professional hiker Glinda knows the location of both and what they identify.

"The marker out at the park entrance tells about the JA Ranch," she says. "And the other one's at the turnaround at the far end of the road. It tells about the Battle of Palo Duro."

"Good," Ranger Burns says. "Who owned the JA Ranch?"

"Charles Goodnight and John Adair," Glinda says.

I raise my hand. "Is that old house up on the rim part of the ranch?"

Ranger Burns frowns. "How'd you know about that?"

Uh-oh, I think. Dad could get in trouble if I tell her he took me there—and she finds out he climbed down the rim.

"Well, see, Dad told me all kinds of things when he

was showing me around. You know, about settlers and Indians and . . . stuff."

"I see." She nods. "It's quite possible, I suppose. Some of the ranch has been sold off, not nearly as big as when Goodnight operated it." She looks around the table again. "And the battle?"

"Indians," X says. "I read about that at the Interpretive Center. The army killed their horses, that's how they were able to capture the Indians."

"So they could move them to reservations in Oklahoma." Ranger Burns shakes her head. "Not everything that's been done here's to be proud of. Okay, look at the last part."

> Name the famous natural landmark that everyone wants to see in Palo Duro Canyon State Park.

"Oh, I know it—I know this one." Everyone looks at me. "The Lighthouse! It's over three hundred feet tall and you're supposed to use the trail in the park to reach it, not climb down from the rim."

Ranger Burns blinks slowly. "Something else you learned from your dad?"

"Um, yes, ma'am. He's very thorough."

"Isn't he, though . . . ," she murmurs.

CHAPTER THIRTEEN

At high noon, Ranger Burns sends us outside to eat. After lunch, she's taking us to the Interpretive Center, which we're expected to learn "upside down and inside out," and after that, on a short hike.

Mr. García is dropping Héctor off at the curb as we walk out the front door. We gather at a picnic table under a cottonwood tree, where shade and breeze make it cooler. I search my bag for something cold to drink and find a bottle of springwater. Lukewarm.

"Some vacation, huh?" Bobby Ray says, opening his lunch. "Homework already."

"Yeah," I mumble. "I hate this place. And Warden Winnie's a real dragon."

"Well, aren't you a fun-filled little lollipop," Glinda says, smirking.

The rest of them laugh. I don't see anything funny.

"Warden Winnie . . . I like it." Bobby Ray unloads his lunch bag. Two sandwiches, three bags of chips—one potato, one corn, one veggie—a banana, a Baggie stuffed with cookies and two diet sodas.

"*Wow.*" Héctor's eyes open wide. "You going to eat all them chips?" His sack holds a sandwich, two sugar-wafer cookies and a bottle of water.

"*Those* chips," X says. "And don't ask things like that. You want people to think we can't buy food?"

"Want some?" Bobby Ray tosses the bag of potato chips to Héctor. "I brought extra."

"*Sí, me gusta* chips."

"In English, Héctor. In *English,*" X says. "You talk like a *burro.*"

Héctor rolls his eyes at X, then turns to Bobby Ray. "Yes," he says, speaking slowly. "I-like-potato-chips." Ripping the bag open, he reaches in for a chip.

"No, *stop.*" X jerks the bag away and tosses it back to Bobby Ray. "We don't take handouts."

Héctor's face clouds up and his eyes turn liquid.

"Hey, man, it's not like that," Bobby Ray says. "*Honest.* I mean, look at me. If I don't lose some weight, I'll never get a girlfriend—a *real* girlfriend. Girls don't like fat boys, even smart fat boys. They pretend they're your friend until you finish their homework, then it's Splitsville."

"*Splitsville?*" Glinda says.

"Yeah. What's wrong with that? My grandpa says that all the time."

Glinda rolls her eyes.

Bobby Ray picks up another bag of chips. "See, I'm eating this kind." He tears open the veggie chips. "Mom buys these 'cause they're low in calories, but they're not bad. Cookies are the diet kind, too." He sighs as he munches.

"One of these days, I'm going to be a smart skinny boy—and popular."

"Right," Glinda snorts. "And I'm going to be tall."

The others laugh at her. I don't get it. They act like Glinda's just horsing around, but I know she's not.

"So you're smart, huh?" X looks at Bobby Ray.

"Very. I even tutor high school kids in math. Algebra's my favorite. You know, equations and stuff? I'm really good at it. It's 'cause I'm fat. Fat kids have fatter brain cells, that's what makes us smarter."

Everyone laughs again, except me. I'm thinking about what Bobby Ray said.

"Maybe it's just because you have more time to study since you don't have friends." I rake crumbs onto the ground for the birds that have shown up. "Doesn't necessarily mean you're extra smart."

"She's right." Glinda looks at me, her eyebrows raised a notch. "Some kids are always trawling for a desperate dink to do their homework. Doesn't matter if you're fat or skinny, short or tall. Maybe the dumb ones are really the smart ones."

I finger the ends of my dip-dyed hair.

"Well," Bobby Ray says, munching diet cookies, "I still think it's better to be skinny and stupid than fat and smart."

"C'mon, Héctor—let's go." X crumples his lunch bag and tosses it like a basketball into a trash can. He heads toward the front of the building, walking fast. Stuffing his bag into the can, Héctor trots after him.

"Huh," Bobby Ray says, watching them go. "How 'bout them apples?"

"Yeah, what got into him?" I say.

"Eat fast, Romeo." Glinda folds her lunch bag into her hip pocket and starts after X. "Looks like lunch is over."

I look at Bobby Ray. "You guys always do what X says?"

"No . . . yeah . . . well, pretty much, I guess. Never thought about it." He scrapes crumbled chips into a pile and tosses it to the birds. "So you're smart, too, huh?"

"Me? *No.* I mean, I *do* study a lot, but I have friends."

At least I *hope* Mandy and Beth are my friends. . . .

He sighs as he dumps his trash. "And I bet you don't even have to do their homework."

CHAPTER FOURTEEN

The Interpretive Center is in one of the old stone buildings the Civilian Conservation Corps built in the 1930s. Inside are exhibits, displays and bookshelves. We scatter, looking at different things. I'm looking at pottery fragments in a glass case when I hear Bobby Ray whisper, "*Glinda—over here.*" I ease up behind them.

"Look," he says, showing her a page in a book.

"Let me see," she says, taking the book from him.

"*Shh,*" he whispers, glancing to where Ranger Burns is looking through a glass case.

Peeking over Glinda's shoulder, I see pictures of arrowheads and spear points. "The missing artifacts, is that what they look like?" I ask.

They turn to stare at me, a surprised look on their faces. They were so engrossed in the book they didn't know anyone was behind them.

"Prob'ly." Bobby Ray takes the book from Glinda. "I figure arrowheads all look pretty much the same." He reshelves the book.

"*Sheesh,*" Glinda says. "You could carry something that little in your pocket. No one would ever know it was there."

"Yeah." I shrug. "But that doesn't mean the thief wouldn't *act* suspicious."

They look at me.

"You know, *sneaky.*"

Bobby Ray's eyes get round. "*Yeah.* We could look for sneaky hikers and catch the thief."

"Okay . . ." Glinda looks at me. "What's a sneaky hiker look like?"

"Well, see . . ." I start to fidget with my hair. "I've never been hiking."

Bobby Ray's shoulders wilt. Glinda rolls her eyes. They walk away together, leaving me standing.

After we finish studying the history, wildlife and geology exhibits, Ranger Burns divides us into two teams. X and Glinda are one team. Bobby Ray and me, another. She assigns trails next. X and Glinda get the longer, harder trails. Bobby Ray and I get the shorter, easier ones.

"If they're the A-team"—Bobby Ray points his chin toward Glinda and X—"what's that make Cassie and me?"

"*The Boo-Hoos,*" Glinda whispers.

Ranger Burns raises an eyebrow. "Catch more flies with honey than with vinegar, Glinda."

"Yes, ma'am," she mutters.

"It's just for now." Ranger Burns looks between Bobby Ray and me. "Once you build up your stamina, I'll shuffle the assignments. Any questions?"

"*Oh—*" Glinda's hand pops up. "Can we look for clues? You know, to help catch the thief?"

"*Yeah.*" Bobby Ray nods, all three chins quivering like jelly. "I always wanted to be a crime buster!"

"That's a dumb idea," X says, snickering.

"No, I think it sounds like fun." I give Bobby Ray and Glinda a hopeful look. "I'd like to be a detective, too—"

"Oh, yeah?" X faces me. "As fast as things change here, what kind of clues you think you'd find?"

"X is right," Ranger Burns says. "Hard to track anything here because of the wind, the loose sandy soil. Besides, you're here to be guides, not detectives."

"That sucks." Glinda slumps in her chair, a balloon deflating. "This summer's not going to be any different than the others. *Bor . . . ing.*"

"Don't worry, Glinda. I'll make sure you don't get bored." Ranger Burns glances down at her notes again. "And Héctor will team with Cassie and Bobby Ray on the hikes." She glances at me. "Saw your dad at lunch and he said you prefer to be called Cassie."

"*No.*" X sits up straight, back stiff. "Héctor has to stay with me. I'm in charge of him when Papá's not around."

He's in charge? I realize I haven't seen Héctor and X's mother. I wonder if she's dead or if their parents are divorced, like mine.

Ranger Burns knots her arms across her chest. "When he's here, *I'm* in charge of him, just as I am with the rest of you. I'm putting him with Bobby Ray and Cassie because the trails are shorter and he'll have a chance to rest more often." She leans forward, facing X squarely. "You see a problem with my thinking?"

"Guess not," he mumbles.

"Good. And as sensitive as Cassie is to the dangers out there"—she waves a hand toward the canyon—"she'll make sure he doesn't get hurt." She looks at me. "Right, Cassie?"

"Yes, ma'am," I say, shoulders drooping.

She thinks I'm a wimp. . . .

"All right then. Just time enough for a short hike. Pile in my patrol car and we'll take off." She walks toward a government-green SUV in the parking lot. "We'll do the Paseo del Rio. It's an easy two-miler, round-trip."

"Don't forget to look for animal prints and scat while you're hiking," Ranger Burns says as we start the hike. "You'll get asked about that, too."

I look at her. "Scat?"

"Animal poop. When other signs are vague, you can identify an animal by its scat."

I had to ask.

Parking off the road, Ranger Burns takes the lead. The A-team follows next, then Bobby Ray. I'm dead last. The trail is fairly flat, but my new boots are stiff and my socks slide down at the heel.

"Keep up, Cassie," Ranger Burns yells.

"Need to fix my shoe." I sit down on a low boulder.

"Well, while you're sitting there, see if you can spot a Texas horned lizard."

I leap off the rock. "Wait up—"

Scat is a big deal. Resuming our hike, we learn that deer leave pills, little brown balls that scatter on the ground. Raccoon scat is full of seeds. Coyote scat is full of hair. I'm grossed out by the time we reach the water crossing where the trail ends.

While the others explore the stream bank, I sit down on a rock to adjust my boots again. One sock feels sticky.

"Cassie . . ." Ranger Burns starts back up the trail, the others dogging her heels. "Rattlers like to sun on the rocks. Hope you looked before you planted your butt there."

"*Hold up.* I'm coming."

Lessons resume when I catch up. "That was water crossing number two back there," Ranger Burns says. "How many water crossings are there in the park?"

"Six," Glinda says.

"Yeah . . . yeah," I grumble. Both heels feel like ground hamburger. My leg muscles ache. I'm tired of listening to the same things over and over. "And they flood fast . . . and a storm can be on you before you know it . . . and because the walls are so high, you won't see it coming."

Ranger Burns eyes me, eyebrows knotted. "You get that from that tour your dad gave you?"

"Um, yes, ma'am. He's, uh, he's a very cautious person."

"Pays to be cautious," she says.

"Where's my dad, Mr. García?" I was the first one out the door at four o'clock. Dad isn't there to pick us up. Mr. García is our taxi instead.

"He had something to take care of." Noticing that I'm limping, Mr. García says, "Why don't you sit up front with me."

"Thanks." I hobble to his truck.

"Me, too, Papá?" Héctor asks.

"Of course, *m'ijo*. Plenty of room for you."

As Héctor squeezes in beside me, I whisper, "Is that your middle name? *Miho?*"

"No." He giggles. "It means 'my son.' I help you with Spanish, you help me with English. Okay?"

"Deal." I grin, giving him a knuckle bump.

We take off as soon as the others are settled in the back end. I'm aching to get back to the Winnebago, but Mr. García drives even slower than Dad.

"What did my dad have to do, Mr. García?"

"Some business. He will be back before dark."

The drive to the Mesquite seems to take forever. Because of the canyon walls, the sun disappears early. Cottonwood trees make shadows on the road that wriggle like snakes when the wind blows. Other dark snakes wiggle up the canyon walls. Darkness is coming on fast.

Mr. García drops Bobby Ray and Glinda off first, then me. Limping inside, I take off my boots and find blisters on both heels. Big ones. I can't stop the tears as I peel my socks away.

Ti appears next to me, smelling my face.

"It hurts a lot, Ti."

He purrs loud, rubbing against me.

For some reason, I feel better. I curl up on my bed, waiting for Dad to come home. Ti lies on the journal next to me, still purring.

"So, how was your day?" I scratch him behind the ears.

He yawns.

"Pretty boring, huh? Well, mine was kind of interesting. See, someone stole some artifacts."

He looks at me with vacant eyes.

"We wanted to help find the thief, but Warden Winnie wouldn't have it." I sigh loudly. "But how hard could it be? All you have to do is keep track of suspicious behavior and clues, then draw conclusions."

The journal tugs at my eyes like a magnet. Easing it from under Ti, I turn to the first page, which says, *This journal belongs to . . .*

Grabbing my pen, I correct the line to read *Cassie's Detective Journal.*

Ti crawls into my lap, sniffing the journal. Suddenly, he swivels his ears toward the window.

"I heard something, too. What was that? Is Dad home?" I set Ti and the journal back on the shelf. "Maybe I better do this when no one's around."

Ti lies down on the journal, his sightless eyes open wide.

CHAPTER FIFTEEN

"Cassie—open the door."

A pounding sound echoing through the darkness makes me jump and makes Ti dig his hind claws into my leg. Recognizing Dad's voice, I stumble to the door and release the dead bolt I set earlier.

"Why did you lock up?" Dad asks, turning on the light. His hair and clothes are coated with dust. Circles of sweat stain the underarms of his shirt. "And why are you sitting in the dark?" He looks around the Winnebago at the closed blinds.

"I heard something—a noise back there." I point to the back wall.

He frowns. "What did it sound like?"

"Uh, metal, I think . . . yeah, definitely metal."

"More than likely it was raccoons. They come down from the canyons, scavenging for scraps. Need to make sure the lid on the trash barrel is down tight."

"Oh, raccoons." My shoulders slump in relief, then

stiffen again. "But see, I didn't put anything in the trash. And Ti heard it first. He was acting spooky."

"Spooky?"

"Yeah, staring at me, not blinking."

"He's not staring at you, Cassie—he's blind."

"But see, then he started slinking around—close to things. And then I heard that metal sound again. That's when I locked the door and closed the blinds."

"Sounds like he did hear something." Dad blinks slowly. "I'm sure it's nothing, but I'll take a look around."

I hobble from window to window, opening blinds so I can follow the beam from Dad's flashlight. Lighting boulders. The ground. Piercing the blackness. The canyon walls have closed in, making things disappear. I lose sight of him as he walks in front of the Winnebago; then I hear a sound. Something tinny, like metal. A few minutes later, he comes back inside.

"Nothing to worry about. As I said, probably raccoons." He's carrying a manila envelope.

"Where'd that come from? What is it?"

"Paperwork." He carries it to his bedroom and locks it in a desk drawer. He glances toward the kitchen when he returns. "Thought you'd have supper going."

"Supper? I have to cook, too?"

"House rules. I'm an early riser, so I fix breakfast. You have plenty of time after you get in from hiking, so you fix supper." He glances toward my messy bed. "You can't be *that* tired."

"But hiking's hard. I got blisters—*big* ones."

"Show me."

"They popped already." I turn my feet so he can look at the heels.

"Sit down at the table." He retrieves a first-aid kit from the bathroom. After cleaning the blistered places, he covers them with gel lubricant and Band-Aids. Pulling a clean pair of socks from the drawer under the bed, he hands them to me. "So, did you have fun today?"

"Oh, yeah, hiking with blisters is a blast, Dad." I pull the socks on carefully.

He frowns. "Can't believe Winnie let you do that. She's a seasoned trekker. Why would she let you hike with your feet in that condition?"

"I don't know," I say, shrugging.

"I'll have a talk with her tomorrow."

"Wait . . . see, I didn't exactly tell her."

He cocks his head, staring at me.

"She thinks I'm a sissy," I blurt, "because I'm afraid of horned lizards."

"She said that?" The furrow between his eyes deepens.

"Not exactly." I tell him about Ranger Burns's reaction to my question. "I felt really . . ."

" . . . dumb?" He grins. "I felt that way when I started in construction."

"You're supposed to pick them up behind their horns, did you know that?" I demonstrate, holding my fingers like tweezers.

"Since I was five," he says. "Hiking will get better. And you don't start until next week, so your feet will be healed by then."

"Yeah," I sigh, "except I'm supposed to hike my trails this week."

"Which ones?"

"Sunflower, Rojo Grande, the Juniper Trail along the river and the Paseo del Rio. We did that one today. They're all two miles long, round-trip. Me and Bobby Ray are partners. We have to build up our stamina before we're given longer trails."

"Shouldn't take long," he says, returning the first-aid kit to the bathroom.

"Oh, and Héctor's going with us. Because I'm scared of everything, Ranger Burns thinks I'll make sure he won't get hurt."

Dad laughs at that. "Can't fault her logic. Just let the others know you have to hold off a couple of days. They won't mind."

"The others? I'm not going with the others. I thought *we'd* hike the trails together. Just you and me."

"Give them a chance, Cassie," he says, sighing. "They're good kids. The fact that they're volunteering to be trail guides should prove it."

"Yeah, but . . ." A part of me is glad I got the shorter, easier trails, but another part of me resents it. "I'm not as good as them, and . . ." I drop my chin, staring at the floor. "They laugh at me."

"I see. Well, there's only one way to get better." He glances at the training materials on the kitchen table. "Looks like you'll have plenty to do in the meantime."

"I guess. . . ."

"You and Bobby Ray can catch up later this week," he says. "And Héctor can stay here with you while X does his trails. You can help him with his reading. He got pretty bored today."

Cooking *and* babysitting?

"Let me clean up, then we'll get supper going," he says. "And I'll tell you about my phone call to Becky—*Rebecca.*" He glances away, staring at the darkness outside the windows.

My heart starts pounding double-time. "Mom—you talked to Mom?"

Supper is BLT sandwiches, chips and leftover spinach salad that Dad spices up with mandarin oranges, red onion slices and feta cheese. To drink, we have iced tea he made with tea bags in a jar, setting it in the sun to steep.

"What time on Saturday are we calling Mom?"

"Early. We're five hours behind her now. Eight in the morning here is three in the afternoon in Germany. We'll do laundry while we're in town, pick up more groceries."

"What'd she say when you talked to her today? How is she? Did she ask about me?"

"She misses you." He pauses to refill his tea glass. "And she's keeping very busy."

"Is that why you couldn't pick us up today, so you could call Mom? Why couldn't I go?"

"Not exactly. Went into town to e-mail off a job bid. When I got where I had phone reception, there was a message waiting from your mom. So I called her. She couldn't talk long."

"Job bid?"

"It's how I get work," he says. "The state puts jobs up for bid. If your bid's the most reasonable, you get the job."

"Where are you going next?"

"Depends on which one of my bids is accepted. I've put in three, good chance I'll get one of them."

"In Austin?" My heart pounds fast. "Maybe you can drive me home. I'd like that a lot."

He stacks the dishes, carries them to the sink. "I didn't bid on a job in Austin, Cassie."

The pounding in my chest turns to an ache. One or the other parent . . . why am I stuck having just one of them?

"I'll clean up," he says, running hot water in the kitchen sink. "You go let Bobby Ray know you won't be hiking for a couple of days. Wear those pink shoes you brought, tied loose. See if his folks can take you and Bobby Ray hiking on Thursday. To stay on schedule, I need to leave early all this week."

"But Dad—"

"*Go.*" He jerks his head toward the door. "Their camper's the blue-and-white Conestoga, near the entrance." He pauses, smiling. "If Bobby Ray gets ugly with you, just pick him up behind his ears."

"Real funny, Dad."

Outside, the beam from the flashlight punches pinholes in the inky darkness. I walk slowly, listening to every noise. My head bent low, I examine the ground, searching for something that looks like certain pictures in the training guide.

But there's not a single raccoon track to be found anywhere. Or scat.

CASSIE'S DETECTIVE JOURNAL: Entry #1

Suspicious Behavior

1. On the day I arrived, X asked Dad if he found "them" but he didn't he say what "them" was.
2. On the way to training, X rode up front with Dad to talk. I suspect he wanted to talk about "them," but in private.
3. At training, X didn't want to help find the artifact thief when the rest of us did. Why not?

Clues

1. X has tattoos like gang members have. A skull on one arm. A gun and dagger on the other—a bloody dagger.
2. He wears a T-shirt with a warning on the front. Gang members sometimes dress to be intimidating.
3. He bosses the other kids around—just like gang leaders do.
4. Gangs do bad things. Break into cars. Vandalize buildings. Beat up regular kids. Steal things.

Conclusion

"Them" must be the stolen artifacts, which makes X the prime suspect.

CHAPTER SIXTEEN

"When's Héctor coming over?" I slice bananas into bowls of bran flakes as Dad butters whole-wheat toast. "How long will he be here?"

"Depends on when X and Glinda leave to go hiking and which trail they take. Don't worry," he says, a smile showing. "I'm sure they'll be back by lunch, so you don't have to cook for him."

"*Good.*" I make a sour face at him. He laughs.

He and Mr. García leave at seven o'clock, Dad driving his big blue pickup and Mr. García his faded red one. I wash up the dishes, then sit down next to Ti so I can watch for Héctor. Ti suns on his window ledge while I study pictures of animal tracks and scat. Raccoons, opossums, squirrels, skunks, coyotes, bobcats, white-tailed deer . . .

So many animals, so much to remember. And so boring.

Wandering to Dad's bedroom, I explore his bookshelves. I find books about building and electrical wiring, hiking guides with maps. Pausing, I look through books on a lower shelf. Old schoolbooks: social studies, language arts, algebra. I reshelve the schoolbooks, wondering if Dad bought them or if they were left in the trailer.

It's midmorning when Héctor runs toward our camper. X follows him partway, watching until I open the door. After Héctor's inside, X walks toward the circular driveway. I notice he's wearing a backpack. A big backpack.

"What did X take in the pack, Héctor?"

"Water and cookies and stuff." Héctor lays his tote on the kitchen table, next to my study materials. "You have to study, too?"

"Yeah," I grumble, "but I can do that this afternoon. Why don't you read to me now?"

"Okay. Lucas got this for me at the library." Pulling a book from his tote, he pronounces the words in the title slowly. "*Frog and Toad Are Friends*."

Taking the book, I skim through the pages. "You mean, toads and frogs are different? I thought they were the same thing."

Héctor's shoulders fall. "You don't know too much, huh, Cassie?"

"Just read," I sigh.

It turns out Héctor has a lot of library books about frogs and toads. We read them all. He goes home later that afternoon when X returns. Looking through the front door, I see Glinda and Bobby Ray join X and Héctor at their picnic table. Suddenly, X leaves the group. My heart pounds as he walks toward the Winnebago. My tongue freezes as I stare at him through the front screen.

"Sorry about your blisters." He glances toward the

others. “Wanna come over? We’re just hanging out till suppertime.”

“Uh, can’t.” My tongue is thick. My eyes are glued to his tattoos. Picturing a knife cutting into skin. The cuts bleeding. “See, I’m, uh, I’m studying.” I indicate the naturalist guide materials on the kitchen table.

He nods. “Okay, maybe later. We’re making s’mores after supper.”

“Oh, yeah . . . sure . . . maybe.”

The smile disappears. His eyes tell me he knows I won’t be coming. Wordless, he walks back to the group. I see him say something to the others, watch the others look my way, notice that X sits with his back to me.

A vacant spot opens up inside me.

While Dad showers, I fix supper. Canned tomato soup and cold ham sandwiches. Iced tea from a jar. Heating the soup on the kitchen stove makes the camper uncomfortably hot, so we eat outside.

“Hmm,” Dad says, crumbling crackers into the watery soup. “Bet the library has cookbooks.”

Library . . .

“Oh, did you know frogs and toads aren’t the same thing? Héctor’s reading the books you got him at the library. Frogs live close to water and have smooth skins, not bumpy, and their legs are longer for jumping. A toad’s tongue isn’t as long as a frog’s, or sticky, so it has to walk up to its food and cram it in its mouth.”

Dad smiles. “How’s Héctor coming with his reading?”

“Good, real good. Only . . .” I study my soup bowl, then look at him. “He pronounces some of the words funny.”

"English is his second language. Just think how you would feel if you had to read in Spanish."

We turn toward the sound of laughter. X and his gang have congregated at their fire pit. They laugh and joke as they hold long sticks over the fire.

"Sounds like they're having fun," Dad says.

"X told me they're making s'mores," I mumble.

"I keep the makings for s'mores in the kitchen pantry. Go over and join them."

"Don't want to."

That's not true. I would very much like to make s'mores, but with *my* friends.

Dad glances toward the campfire where the gang is gathered. "Sounds like X invited you to join them."

Following his gaze, I see Bobby Ray waving his arms around and hear Glinda laugh. I don't know if X is laughing, because he's sitting with his back to me.

Mandy and Beth and me, I decide. We'll make s'mores as soon as I get back home.

"Why wouldn't you go?" Dad asks.

"Because . . . Well, X is kind of . . . different," I mumble.

"Different," he says. "Like toads and frogs?" Shaking his head, he begins to clear the table.

Dad's not happy with me; I can tell because his mouth is set hard as cement. Why's he always taking X's side?

Is that suspicious behavior . . . ?

CASSIE'S DETECTIVE JOURNAL: Entry #2

Suspicious Behavior

On my first day here when X mentioned "them," Dad knew what he was talking about and where "they" were hidden. Why would he know this?

Clues

1. Ti and I heard a noise outside the camper—a tinny-sounding noise, like metal. Dad said he thought he knew what it was.
2. When he checked the noise, he brought back an envelope, which he locked in his desk.
3. Dad hinted that it doesn't hurt to break a rule now and then—and he broke one when he climbed down to the Lighthouse from the canyon rim. Has he broken other rules?

Conclusions

Dad is definitely X's accomplice. He left his good-paying job, so now he's short of money and has turned to a life of crime. No wonder he didn't want me to know what he was doing!

CHAPTER SEVENTEEN

Wednesday is a repeat of Tuesday. I listen to Héctor read more of *Frogs and Toad Are Friends*. Study my naturalist guide. Think about all the things I wrote in my detective journal last night that prove Dad is X's accomplice. I tell myself over and over that Dad wouldn't . . . he couldn't.

And yet . . .

It's a quiet day, with no wind to speak of. After X returns from his hike and Héctor goes home, the Winnebago is too quiet. My mind, too noisy. I decide to practice my tracking skills.

The sandy soil out back is littered with prints. I examine each one, compare it to pictures in my guide.

Skunk . . . ?

Opossum . . . ?

Squirrel . . . ?

Bobcat—? Would a bobcat come this close to where people live?

My head tells me no. My heart pounding against my

ribs says maybe. I squat on my heels, studying the questionable print closer.

"*Nuts*—it's no use. I'm no good at this."

Scuffing my feet, I return to the camper. Rounding the corner, I stumble onto more tracks. New ones.

"No . . ." The screen door is ajar. "*Oh, no.*"

Fresh cat prints weave through the mesquite and juniper, ending at the bottom of a steep outcropping. Heart pounding, I climb a boulder, looking in every direction. A dark-gray shadow on top of a rocky ledge looks out of place. Ti is stretched out, napping.

He's not scared. Why isn't he afraid?

I inch toward him, not wanting to scare him into running. He hears me coming from a long way off. His eyes open wide. His ears twitch like mad. Slowly, he rises, arching his back.

"It's just me, Ti." I talk quietly, holding my hand out for him to sniff. "I'm picking you up now, so don't bite me."

He lets me hold him close. Sitting down on the boulder, I rub his head.

"Know what I think?" I press my face into the soft fur on his neck. He feels warm, smells of sagebrush and juniper. "I think you like it out here. Maybe Dad's wrong. Maybe you *do* need to get out of the Winnebago sometimes. Maybe we'll get you a collar and leash so I can take you for walks. What do you think of that?"

He purrs.

The rock is warm. The sun is brilliant. The rocks are desert red, the mesquite and yucca sage green.

"It's not such a bad place, is it? Once you get used to the sand and flies . . . *and* things prowling around in the dark—"

Suddenly, Ti's ears swivel toward the ground. My heart pounds as something wriggles past my feet. I freeze, squeezing him tighter. "Look," I whisper. "It's a horned lizard."

The squatty little lizard looks like a miniature dinosaur. Wide and flat, with a stumpy tail and a bony ridge—its horns—over black BB eyes.

"You think I should . . . ?" Holding Ti in the crook of one arm, I pick the lizard up behind its horns. "His belly's real soft, Ti, and he's not squirting at us. Want to smell him?"

Making sure the lizard's head is pointed away, I hold it close to Ti. The cat's nose sniffs madly. His tail whips back and forth. Suddenly, the lizard starts squirming, its stubby tail flicking from side to side.

"It's time to turn him loose," I whisper to Ti. The lizard shuffles under a rock after I free it. "And we need to go, too."

CHAPTER EIGHTEEN

At ten o'clock on Thursday morning, I walk to Bobby Ray's camper. Blistered heels protected with Band-Aids and moleskin. A bottle of water and two granola bars in a paper sack.

"Think we should ask Héctor to go with us?" Bobby Ray asks as I walk up. He's wearing a polo shirt and plaid hiking shorts that bunch up between his thighs. A large backpack hangs from one shoulder.

"Why do you need that?" I point at the backpack.

"To carry stuff. Give me your sack, I'll carry it for you. Don't you have a pack?"

"All I brought is a day pack."

"That'll do. You need to keep your hands free when you hike. Never know when you might trip—or need to fight off lions and tigers and bears."

He grins. I groan.

"I've been thinking Héctor should come with us," he says, looking toward the Garcías' camper.

"Think X would let him? He's awful bossy."

"X *is* pretty tough on Héctor, but just because he wants to spend his summer reading doesn't mean Héctor does, too."

X spends his time reading . . . ?

"Yeah . . ." I glance toward the Garcías' camper again. "Héctor should prob'ly come."

"You get him. I'll tell Dad we're ready to go."

Bobby Ray's gone before I can protest.

X stands behind their screen door. Arms folded. Eyes cold.

"No," he tells me. "Héctor's going with Glinda and me today. The Juniper-Cliffside's only six miles long, round-trip."

Their camper is smaller than ours, which explains the plastic storage tubs sitting under their picnic table. I figure the tubs get stowed in the back of their pickup when they move somewhere else, or maybe on top of the camper. I eye the tubs closely, thinking they would be a good place to hide something—and sneak that something out of the park.

"We've done longer ones," X goes on. "A lot longer."

"But Ranger Burns assigned him to me," I insist. "Héctor needs to learn *our* trails."

"Yeah," Héctor says, peeking around X's legs. "*Our* trails."

X doesn't budge.

"Look at it this way," I say. "If you let Héctor go with us, you and Glinda can finish sooner so you can do something fun when you get back. You know, like . . . *read.*"

X blinks a few times, then turns to Héctor. "Get your pack," he says.

* * *

Mr. Jones, Bobby Ray's dad, is a skinny man with a stubble of gray hair and bottle-bottom glasses. Dropping us off at the Sunflower Trail, he says, "Pick you up in about an hour. Shouldn't take you more than that."

"Well, see, we're supposed to study tracks and plants," Bobby Ray tells him. "It might take us longer."

"If you're not here, I'll wait till you show up. And wear your hats. Could get sunstroke in this heat."

Sunstroke. Another thing to put on my things-to-worry-about list.

CHAPTER NINETEEN

Bobby Ray leads off the hike on the Sunflower Trail. I bring up the rear. Héctor walks between us. His guardians. The only wildlife we see is lizards, without horns, and birds. But we spot deer tracks and others that could be raccoon, opossum or skunk.

"So, you think a raccoon made it?" I squat on my heels, studying a track. "How can you tell?"

"See, the front toes are long, like fingers. X showed me what they look like."

"And this is its scat." Bobby Ray uses a stick to rake through a pile of poop. "See, it's full of seeds."

"This one is coyote." Héctor points out tracks resembling a medium-sized dog's.

I bend close. "How do you know it's not a bobcat?"

"Bobcat is not so big."

Because his father's a botanist, Bobby Ray's a walking plant encyclopedia. He shows us star thistle, sunflowers, Blackfoot daisies, buffalo grass and prickly pear cactus.

"You can eat those fat-looking pads," he says, pointing to the cactus. "They're called *nopales*. Those red nubs there are the fruit. I guess they taste like pears. Mom won't fix them 'cause they're covered in spines that stab you."

"I show you how to get them." Picking up a long stick, Héctor whacks pads off the cactus.

"Stop, Héctor—*stop*." I grab the stick away from him. "You can't do that."

"But I want to bring some back for Papá like I used to in México."

"The rules are different in a state park," Bobby Ray says, kicking the broken *nopal* pads under a mesquite. "Not supposed to collect plants or nothin'—not even a rock."

"Too many rules," Héctor says, mouth in a pout.

"C'mon, let's take a break." I lead Héctor to a low boulder. "I brought extra granola bars." Before sitting, I check for snakes.

"Yeah, me, too." Bobby Ray plops down on the rock next to us. "I brought plenty of cookies—the diet kind."

"I got cookies." Héctor pulls a sandwich bag filled with homemade oatmeal-raisin cookies from his day pack. "Miss Pearl, she is always making stuff for us."

"Oh, yeah? Wanna swap some?" Bobby Ray pulls the bag of diet cookies from his backpack.

I unwrap a granola bar and watch Bobby Ray and Héctor swap cookies.

"*Uh-oh*." Three cookies later, Bobby Ray starts to fidget. "Back in a minute." Carrying a roll of toilet tissue and a gardening trowel, he trots toward a clump of juniper.

Héctor starts to giggle. "He's gotta go . . . you know."

"Make scat," I say, grinning, too. "Um, so you used to live in Mexico, Héctor?"

"*Sí*, my mother and sisters still live there. We move here so Papá can work and send money back to them."

Send money back? All at once, I'm wondering how much an artifact would sell for.

I look at Héctor again. "Remember on the way to headquarters, when Dad had X sit up front with him?"

He nods.

"Do you know why? What Dad needed to talk to him about, I mean?"

Héctor nods. "But I can't tell you."

"Why not?"

"It's a secret."

Secret . . . Dad *is* keeping a secret.

I hope I'm wrong, but I'm afraid that secret is about those stolen artifacts.

After Bobby Ray and Héctor and I return from hiking, I try out my detective skills, searching for tracks leading to something metal that would make a tinny sound. Studying the ground behind our camper, I find remnants of different kinds of tracks. Coyote. Raccoon. Birds. But they're not what I'm looking for. In front of my eyes, a breeze moves the sand around, scouring the ground clean.

It's hopeless, I think. There's no way a track would survive in the wind here. It's a lunar landscape, scraped clean, just like X said.

Discouraged, I trudge back around the camper. Suddenly, the breeze uncovers an indentation on the ground. Part of a heel print, one with deep ridges.

Heart racing, I make a footprint next to it. The heel print is similar to mine.

A hiking boot?

"It's prob'ly Dad's. He would've left tracks when he was looking around," I whisper to myself.

Hearing Dad's truck, I hurry around front.

"Hey, Peaches—" He stops short, looking at me. "Sorry. I meant to say Cassie."

"It's okay, Dad. Peaches is okay when it's just us."

"Really?" he says, smiling. "That's great. So, how was your day?"

"It was all right. How was yours? Anything . . . new?"

"Nope," he says. "Nothing interesting, anyway."

I glance at his feet, looking for a track like the one I found out back. His leather work boots are worn down at the heel, leaving a smooth print different from the one I found. And a lot larger.

So that other track means there *was* someone else here that night, who deliberately left that envelope for Dad to find. And *that* means . . .

The word *accomplice* echoes through my head, again and again.

"What is it, Peaches?" Dad looks at me, frowning. "Blisters hurting?"

"Uh, no. They're, uh, they're better."

"Good. Pearl stopped me on the way in. Said for you to come over and she'd teach you a recipe."

"I'll go now."

"No need to rush off. Day's young, and I'd like to hear about your hike. . . ."

I hurry away, not knowing what to say to my dad. One word has changed everything.

Accomplice.

CHAPTER TWENTY

"You see how I'm doing it?" Pearl asks.

I watch her use a stick to move large pieces of burning wood to the side of their fire pit.

"I started these pieces of charcoal earlier, see how they've turned gray? All you do now is level them out so your pot will sit even." She uses the stick to scoot the coals around. "Then you make a hole the size of your Dutch oven. Soon as we set the pot in it, we'll pull some of the coals around it so it cooks through."

"Wow, that fire's really hot." I pull back from the campfire, cheeks scorched.

"Pot holders keep your hands from getting burned. You'll learn quick enough not to lean too close. Now . . ." She walks me toward her camper door. "Let's get the stew going."

I open two cans of white beans and two cans of chick-peas while Pearl chops vegetables.

"Use that colander to rinse and drain the beans," Pearl

says. She's slicing Italian sausages into chunks. "Dump them into the pot with these sausages. I use cooked sausage. If you use uncooked sausage, you'll need to fry it first. Now we'll add some olive oil, these chopped bell peppers . . ." Red and green chunks of pepper go into the pot with the beans and sausages. "And some herbs and spices. Chopped rosemary, a few cloves of chopped garlic and a poblano chili—take out the seeds if you don't like your food hot. I like to spice up things a little. Life gets too dull, you don't kick it up a little."

The lid makes a metallic *clank* when Pearl puts it on the Dutch oven.

I lift the lid and replace it, listening to the sound.

"Something wrong?" Pearl asks, watching me.

"No, just making sure the lid's on good and tight."

"Okay then, that's it," she says, picking up the pot. "Just need to take it outside."

I hold the door open for her and watch as she nestles the pot into its bed of hot coals.

"Takes about forty-five minutes. Best to take the lid off every fifteen minutes or so to see how it's doing. You have some fresh oregano on hand, toss in about a quarter cup near the end."

"Oregano?"

"It's an herb." She studies me closely. "Think you can handle it?"

"Well, it *is* kind of hard." I look toward the Winnebago. "And I don't think Dad has all those things."

"Recipes don't need to be exact, Cassie," she says. "That's what makes cooking fun. Just scrounge through your pantry and use what you have on hand. Kind of like life, you know."

* * *

I let the others talk during supper. I learn that Dad's work is going well and he should finish on schedule. Charlie helped some new campers with their awning, which got stuck halfway down. And Pearl broke up a squabble between five-year-old twins that started because one thought the other's cookie was bigger. To questions about my blisters, which Dad brings up, I say, "They're healing fine."

For dessert, Pearl brings out oatmeal-raisin cookies.

Refilling coffee cups, Dad asks, "Any more on the pilfering, Charlie?"

I glance his way, thinking about the secret he's keeping. Trying to stop the question that nags me.

He wouldn't break the law . . . would he? He *did* climb down the rim illegally, but that isn't as bad as stealing. . . .

"I heard nothin' new," Charlie says.

"Me, either." Stirring milk into her cup, Pearl looks at me. "You've hardly said a word all evening, Cassie. Something troubling you?"

Everyone looks at me, waiting.

"What's up, Cassie?" Dad says, frowning. "Something on your mind?"

"No, nothing. . . ."

All at once, I start wondering if I could make someone let something slip. If I could pick up another clue.

"Well, see, I was just wondering what someone would do with old arrowheads. I mean, are Plano points worth a lot of money? Who would buy something like that?"

"*Plano* points?" Charlie raises his eyebrows. "So that's what the thieves took? Probably some collectors would be mighty happy to get their hands on Plano points."

"How many they take?" Pearl asks.

"Three. They disappeared from a dig site. One of the archaeologists discovered them missing."

"How'd you know that, Cassie?" Dad looks at me, his frown deeper.

"Ranger Burns told us. She said they were five thousand years old."

"My . . . *my*," Pearl says. "Those could be worth a pretty penny, if you could find the right buyer."

"Five thousand years old, huh?" Dad says, rubbing his chin.

"Well now," Pearl says, patting my hand. "That's the best chatter I heard all day."

"Time to turn in, Cassie," Dad says. "You've got an early hike."

"But—"

Dad points his chin toward our camper.

Great detective work, I think as I walk to the Winnebago. All I've learned is that the stolen points are valuable—which is a solid motive.

More clues. I need more clues.

CASSIE'S DETECTIVE JOURNAL: Entry #3

Suspicious Behavior

1. Héctor knows what the secret is that Dad and X are keeping, but he can't tell. Why not?
2. Héctor said he and X are expected to help make money for their family back in Mexico.
3. Dad brought up the stolen points during supper and was very interested in how much they would sell for.

Clues

1. Big backpacks aren't clues, it's just what hikers wear. But what does X use his for?
2. All kinds of things make tinny sounds, even Dutch ovens. What else makes tinny sounds?
3. The Garcías have lots of big storage tubs. And I bet Warden Winnie would never search them because the Garcías are longtimers, just like us and Glinda and Bobby Ray's parents. And Warden Winnie trusts longtimers.
4. X said that he and Héctor had hiked some of the trails, including long ones. The Lighthouse Trail is one of the longest, and you can climb down the rim to get there. I know because Dad showed me the way.

Conclusion

1. I need to locate the dig site where the points were stolen, find out if it's near the Lighthouse Trail.
2. And I need to find out if X hiked the Lighthouse Trail just before the artifacts disappeared.

CHAPTER TWENTY-ONE

"What trail today?" Mr. Jones asks on Friday morning. He's going to drive Bobby Ray and me to our trail again.

Bobby Ray looks at me. "You choose, Cassie."

"The Lighthouse," I say quickly.

"*Lighthouse?*" Bobby Ray looks at me like I've gone loopy. "That's one of X's and Glinda's trails. Besides, we still have to do the Juniper-Riverside and the Rojo Grande."

"Okay. Let's do them both today."

"*Both* of them?" He gives me another loopy look.

"Yeah, then we can do the Lighthouse. I'll go get Héctor."

"Wait up, he's not coming."

"Why not?"

"He has to get his school vaccinations."

"They're going to school here?"

"Sounds like it." Bobby Ray gives me a sideways look. "You'd *know* these things if you came over in the evenings."

I ignore his sarcasm. "But that means Héctor will miss out on one of his trails."

Bobby Ray shrugs. "He and X have already done a lot of them."

"Don't think we have time for two hikes today anyway." Mr. Jones's bottle-bottom glasses make his eyes huge. "The missus made plans for this afternoon, and I'm her chauffeur."

"Yay for Mom," Bobby Ray says. "Okay, then"—he looks at me—"*I'm* choosing. We're doing the Juniper-Riverside 'cause it's the flattest. Okay?"

I nod, sighing.

I'm getting nowhere. . . .

We finish the hike fast because the Juniper-Riverside *is* flat. And boring. The only trail that interests me now is the Lighthouse.

That night after supper, I watch Dad working in his bedroom for a while, then walk to his doorway.

"What're you working on?"

He looks at me over his reading glasses. "Bookwork. Have to keep track of expenses and salaries."

"This job's a lot different than the one you had in Austin, isn't it?"

"Yep," he says, looking down at his paperwork. "I was a little fish in a big pond in Austin." He looks up at me, his eyes twinkling. "Now I'm a big fish in a little pond."

"You, uh, you making a lot of money? You know, like before?"

"Nope," he says, looking down at his ledger again. "But I'll take this any day."

Leaving Dad to his bookwork, I sit down in front of the storm door. Feeling Ti rub against my arm, I describe what I see to him.

"Fire pits are sending up a lot of smoke and sparks . . . like sparklers on the Fourth." I look at the sky. "And there's a gazillion stars out."

Ti turns his head toward a sound. X's gang is at their fire pit. Hearing laughter, I wonder if they're talking about Warden Winnie . . . or me.

A lump fills my throat. I feel like crying.

The cries of coyotes ricocheting around the canyon make Ti tense.

"It's okay," I murmur, holding him close. "You're safe here."

Why don't *I* feel safe?

I glance toward Dad's door.

CHAPTER TWENTY-TWO

Saturday morning. Seven o'clock. I'm dressed, ready to go call Mom.

"Only a twenty-, thirty-minute drive, Peaches. No need to rush." Dad strips the sheets off my bed. "Put your dirty clothes in this pillowcase."

"But we have to call Mom at eight." I stuff the pillowcase with dirty shirts and shorts, socks and underwear. "There might be a traffic jam. We could get a flat tire."

"You're being a worrywart. Soon as we reach the top, we'll call your mom. Do our laundry and grocery shopping later."

He pulls some index cards from his shirt pocket. "Pearl copied these recipes off for you, said they were easy to make." He flips through the cards. "Looks like we'll be eating pretty well . . . for a change." He grins at me.

I fake a smile. The last thing on my mind is cooking.

As Dad hauls our laundry out to the truck, I brush my hair for the third time. I know it's dumb, but I want to look good when I talk to Mom.

"How do I look, Ti?"

He yawns, showing a mouthful of razor-sharp teeth.

"I know, but it's the best I could do. Dad's shampoo, remember? And no conditioner."

He curls up on the journal, purring.

"Let's go, Cassie!" Dad calls.

"Coming!"

As we pull away, X comes out of their camper. Watching him in the side mirror, I see him angle toward the Winnebago.

Where's he going? I bet it's to that place . . . the place he puts things for Dad.

Which means the secret is very close.

Dad stops near some towers alongside the road after we get out of the canyon. A good spot for cell phone reception. He punches a number in his speed dial and hands the phone to me.

"Mom? Yeah, I can hear you fine."

"How are you, Cassie? Are you having fun? I hope you're writing in your journal. I can hardly wait to hear everything you've been doing."

Journal. She'd be surprised to know it's now my detective journal.

"Well, see," I say into the phone, "I'm training to be a guide for the Junior Naturalist Program. So I've been real busy."

"That's wonderful! Your dad arranged that for you? It's the kind of thing he's interested in. I bet you're making a lot of new friends, too."

"Sort of. But I miss Mandy and Beth."

A pause comes on the line. "They're the girls who talked you into dyeing your hair, aren't they?"

"Yeah, them. So, how is it? You seeing lots of old castles and stuff?"

She laughs. "No time for that yet. It's nose to the grindstone right now. But I've been thinking that maybe we can do the tourist thing together. You'd like that, wouldn't you?"

"Come see you in Europe! That would be great. When? You're only there a few more weeks."

"Not so fast," she says, laughing again. "I'm still working things out. Nothing's definite yet, but it's looking promising. We'll talk about it in a couple of weeks, okay?"

I look at Dad. "She wants us to call her again two weeks from today." When he nods, I say, "Same time?"

"I have it on my calendar. Need to go to a meeting now. Love you, Cassie."

"Love you, too."

I listen to a *click*, hear a buzzing on the line and hand the phone to Dad.

"Sounds like that went well," he says, starting the truck. "She finalized plans for you to go over there?"

I stare at him. "You knew about that?"

"She mentioned it when we talked."

I notice he's not smiling. "You don't like the idea much, do you, Dad?"

He stares at the road ahead. "It would be a good educational opportunity for you."

"Yeah, but it's not definite yet. She sounds pretty busy."

"She does like to keep busy," he says.

* * *

"Here we go." Dad turns into a parking lot where a sign says LAUNDROMAT. He pauses before opening his door. "You want, you can call your friends on the way back to the campsite."

"Beth and Mandy?" I feel a flutter in my stomach.

"Bet you know their numbers by heart."

I do know their numbers. But as I think about it, I wonder what I'd tell them. "Probably not a good idea to tell them about Europe yet. . . ."

"Probably not," he says.

That leaves horned lizards, bobcats and blisters, I think.

"Well, see . . ." I glance at Dad. "They sleep in on weekends and will probably go to the mall later. They spend a lot of time there."

"Dip-dying their hair?" he says, chuckling.

Hair . . .

"*Oh,* can we get some conditioner at the grocery store? One that doesn't attract flies?"

"Bet we can find something that'll work."

CHAPTER TWENTY-THREE

Finding ingredients for Pearl's recipes takes a long time. Most of them are cooked in aluminum foil, which will be easier than using a Dutch oven. Apples by the Fire, Grilled Chicken Packets, Baked Potatoes, Hobo Stew. Even a recipe for a no-bake cookie.

I groan as Dad picks up a large bag of spinach.

"I promised your mom," he says.

"Then can we get some mandarin oranges to go with it?"

"You got it."

In the canned goods section, he also picks up canned peaches, apricots, beans and evaporated milk. "Always good to keep nonperishables on hand," he says. "Anything else we need?"

"Um, maybe we could buy Ti a collar and leash. I'd like to take him for walks."

He smiles. "You bet." After we pick out a leash and collar, he says, "Is that it?"

I feel the tips of my hair. Coarse as straw. "Just conditioner."

We take a long time reading the backs of labels to find a conditioner that's not scented like flowers or fruit. By the time we add cat food and litter for Ti, the basket is overflowing.

"Need to pull the camper across the road to the dump station this afternoon," Dad says as we load grocery bags into the truck. "On the way back to the Mesquite, pick a recipe you want to fix tonight. We'll keep out what you need, store the rest."

"Dump station? What do you need to dump?"

"Gray and black water, from the kitchen and bathroom."

"So, gray water's from the sinks and black water's from the . . ."

"Right."

"Gross."

"Not a fun job, that's for sure."

Oh . . . The reason Dad uses the bathhouse shower at the Mesquite suddenly becomes clear. It's so he doesn't have to go to the dump station as often.

"Hold up, Dad. I need one more thing." I stick out my hand, palm up. "A ten should cover it."

"What?" he says, taking out his wallet.

"Picture's worth a thousand words," I say, hopping out of the truck. I hate the idea of using the community shower, but if I shower where the others do, I might pick up more clues.

CHAPTER TWENTY-FOUR

Chicken and Potato Foil Packs are on the menu for supper.

"Looks like you're cutting the recipe in half," Dad says, laying two skinless breasts, two potatoes, an onion, a green pepper and some button mushrooms on a cutting board on the picnic table. "That's a good idea. Pearl always cooks for a crowd."

I add the remaining ingredients to his pile. Vegetable oil, cider vinegar, garlic powder, black pepper, salt, basil and thyme.

"Sure you don't need my help?" Dad says, eyeing the stack.

"I get stuck, I'll go get Pearl."

"How about I leave Ti with you for company? Be a good time to try out that new leash."

"Yeah, I'd like that."

Dad returns with Ti. Securing the end of the leash to a table leg, he walks to the camper to hook it to the truck.

Ti lifts his nose, sniffing the breeze. His ears swivel like tiny radar dishes. Hearing a tinny-sounding *clink*, he turns his ears in the direction it came from.

That's *it*, I think, looking in the same direction. The sound we heard that night.

Dad's standing near the hitch, in front of a small red toolbox behind the propane tank. Just as I reach him, he pulls a tattered manila envelope from the box.

"What's that, Dad?"

He turns to face me. "Nothing to worry about." Folding the envelope, he slips it into his hip pocket. "Need anything from the camper before I haul it to the dump station?"

Shaking my head, I walk back toward the picnic table. Pausing, I stare at a set of footprints, not yet windblown.

"What're you looking at?"

"What—?" Startled, I look toward the front of Dad's truck and see X watching me. "What're you doing here, X?"

"He's going with me." Dad walks up to us. "We'll be gone about an hour, maybe less."

"Oh, okay." I wait, watching them finish up. When they pull away, they're bending each other's ears about something, faces looking serious.

What . . . ? What are they talking about?

As soon as they're out of sight, I retrieve Ti and return to the footprints. Making a print from my own boot alongside one of them, I stoop to examine it.

"Hiking boot," I whisper. "See the tread? Just like the prowler left back of the Winnebago." I look at Ti. "It's him, no guessing anymore. X is the prowler. But what are they hiding in those envelopes?"

* * *

I set Ti on the picnic table and talk to him as I start a fire. Wood first, then charcoal briquettes.

"Okay, let's review. Here's what we know. Someone came prowling around the camper and he wore hiking boots. We both heard him. *That* would be X."

Ti starts to purr.

"Good, we agree." Returning to the table, I pinch the edges of the foil together. "And the toolbox is the 'usual place' that X mentioned on that first day. And the envelopes are the 'them' he was talking about." I look at Ti. "But what's X putting in those envelopes? Arrowheads? And why does Dad give them back to him? Payment?"

Ti purrs.

"You think Dad's planning to haul the Plano points out of the park? All kinds of ways to hide things in construction stuff . . . wait, that doesn't make sense."

I rub my face, then look at Ti. "Why Dad and not Mr. García? He has construction stuff, too, and big storage containers."

To throw Warden Winnie off the trail? a voice in my head whispers.

His ears swiveling, Ti seems to look away. Following him, I see two squirrels fussing over an empty nutshell.

"It's called a red herring," I say to Ti. "Crooks lay down a false trail to mislead the cops." I pause, thinking. "Or, maybe because his English isn't so good, Mr. García would have a harder time trying to sell them, so Dad's fencing the stolen loot."

In my head, it makes sense. But in my heart . . .

"Dad wouldn't do anything *real* bad, would he, Ti? I know he's really changed, but still . . ."

Ti starts to purr again.

I stoke up the fire and place the foil packets on graying coals. Returning to the table, I look at Ti again. "But if it's nothing bad, why's he keeping it a secret?"

Dad returns as I'm setting the table for supper. X leaves immediately, the manila envelope visible in his back pocket.

As Dad unhooks the camper, I whisper to Ti. "We need more clues. We need to make sure we're absolutely right before we confront Dad."

My heart feels like a leaden lump in my chest. I never dreamed I'd be looking for ways to prove my dad was a thief.

CHAPTER TWENTY-FIVE

"Do the showers have doors on them?" My new flip-flops slap the ground like seal flippers. Dad was surprised when I walked out of the grocery store with them, but I could tell he was pleased.

"Don't know about the women's," he says. "Men's don't." He stops outside the entrance marked WOMEN. "Leave those bandages on your heels. We'll change them back at the camper. Meet you out here."

Looking at the building, I heave a sigh. Sturdy cement blocks. Government-gray paint. Musty smells. I envision plugged toilets. Rusty pipes and mildew. A group shower where everyone stands naked under sputtering showerheads.

Someone passes me, her flip-flops slapping the cement floor.

"There's doors," Glinda says, disappearing inside.

How does she do that? How does she know what I'm thinking?

Glinda disappears behind a shower door. Walking into the stall next to her, I hang my towel and tote on a hook.

"That you?" she asks through the metal wall.

"Yep, Miss Nosy Butt."

A soft laugh floats underneath the partition.

"Hey, look," I say. "I'm really sorry about staring at you when we first met. I don't do dumb things *all* the time."

Silence.

I soap up, then rinse off.

"Better angle the nozzle down or you'll drown your tote," Glinda says.

She has X-ray vision, too?

"Thanks." Adjusting the showerhead, I lather shampoo into my hair, then rinse it out.

"What, uh, what do you use on your hair?" she asks. "You know, to make it soft?"

"Oh. See, that was my old conditioner, but I can't use it because it draws flies." I squirt some of the new conditioner into my hand and rub it in. "So I bought some new stuff because my hair's getting real dry."

"It's the wind and sun," she says. "They strip the oils out."

An image of Glinda's hair pops into my head. Dry yellow corn husks.

"Want to try it?" I set the conditioner on the floor between our stalls. "Doesn't smell as good as my old stuff, but even unscented is better than nothing."

Short, tanned fingers pick up the bottle. It reappears a minute later.

"You like it?"

She mumbles, "*Mmm . . .* "

Hearing the water shut off in her shower, I shut mine off, too. Time to turn detective. "You, uh, you hike with X today?"

"No, they go to town on Saturdays. Besides, we're all done. We didn't do the Lighthouse Trail because he did it already. And I've done it umpteen times."

X *has* hiked the Lighthouse. . . .

"Um, yeah. Bobby Ray and I aren't doing the Paseo del Rio again, either. You know, the one Ranger Burns took us on that first day? We did the Sunflower yesterday." I hesitate. "What, uh, what do you and X talk about on those long hikes?"

"What did you and Bobby Ray talk about?" Her words sound muffled, like something's covering her face.

I pull a clean tee over my head. "He's really good with plants, and Héctor knows all about tracks. I don't know anything about anything."

Another laugh.

Hearing her door open, I open mine, too. With her hair stuck close to her head, Glinda looks like a blond elf.

"Ever think about getting a pixie cut? My mom wears her hair in a pixie. She's petite, like you."

Glinda raises her eyebrows. "Petite?"

"Yeah, she's shorter than I am. I take after my dad. You could wear a pixie, too."

She towel-dries her hair back into its rumpled look. Only now it looks softer.

"Same with us," she says, flip-flopping to the door. "Plants and tracks."

The sound of flip-flops dies away.

Great detective work, the voice in my head whispers.

"Oh, no . . ." An unexpected sight makes me stop outside the bathhouse. "What's *she* doing here?"

Ranger Burns is parked on the circular drive, talking

with Dad. Easing up behind them, I listen in on their conversation.

“ . . . Just got a lot on my mind, Lucas,” Ranger Burns tells him. “Sorry, I didn’t pick up on it.”

“I understand,” Dad says. “Must not’ve found those missing Plano points yet. Else you wouldn’t be working on a Saturday.”

“How’d you know they were Plano?” she asks, frowning.

“I told him.” I step forward quickly. “You didn’t say it was a secret. Is it a secret?”

“Guess I didn’t at that,” she says. “But it’s probably best you don’t broadcast it. Tell the others to keep their mouths shut, too.”

“Why?”

“You could alert the thieves,” she says.

Too late, I think.

Ranger Burns faces Dad again. “Working today because we’re shorthanded, Lucas. Training classes starting up soon, hope to get a new ranger trainee assigned here. In the meantime, I’m pulling extra duty. Decided to ask around, see if Charlie or Pearl noticed anyone acting suspicious.” She pauses, scratching behind one ear. “My gut tells me those points are still here somewhere. Lots of people coming in but few are leaving, and we’re searching everything. Someone’s bound to slip up, brag or show them off to their buddies.”

“Well,” Dad says, “can’t speak for the other campground hosts, but Charlie and Pearl don’t miss much.”

“They’re top-notch, all right. Well, best be off.”

“*Wait.*” I step closer. “That dig site where those archaeologists are working, where is it?”

"Well, now," she says, "there's more than one dig going on, but probably best not to discuss the locations. Can tell you why the Indians chose this place, though. It was because of the jasper."

"Makes sense," Dad says. "Jasper's a hard stone, good for making arrowheads and spear points."

Ranger Burns looks at my feet, then my face. "Next time, you tell me when you're getting blisters. You can't do the guide program, I'll understand."

"No—I can do it." Hiking the trails has suddenly become very important to me. "Dad fixed the blisters. The skin's gotten really tough. He knows how to do things like that."

"Yes," she says. "Your dad's very knowledgeable about a lot of things."

A lot of things? What's that mean? Does she suspect Dad, too?

X and the others are gathering at the fire pit.

"Cassie—come over," Bobby Ray yells.

"Can't," I yell back. "Stuff to do."

I hang my towel in the bathroom to dry, then walk to where Ti is curled up on the journal.

I glance out the front door, looking toward Charlie and Pearl's camper. "Warden Winnie is snooping around. I think she suspects Dad of being the thief. You think she'll search the campers? Gosh, we can't let her find anything incriminating."

I look toward Dad's bedroom. "You listen for Dad. I'll be right back."

Dad's desk drawers won't open. Searching the top of the desk, I don't find a key.

"Still locked." I sit down cross-legged next to Ti. "He's hiding something for sure."

Getting up off the journal, Ti inches his way across my bed, then drops to the floor. I watch as he feels his way to Dad's room. Leaping onto the bed, he curls up on a mat Dad keeps for him. His vacant eyes find me, then close slowly.

"Are you giving up? But you can't, Ti. We *have* to find the evidence and get rid of it before it incriminates him."

Ti's eyes pop open as I hear footsteps on the front stoop.

"Don't worry," I whisper, glancing his way. "I know someone who knows what the secret is. And I'm going to squeeze it out of him."

Dad is quiet as he puts a new dressing on my heels. Try as hard as I might, I can't help but fidget.

He looks up at me. "You're flighty as a butterfly on a leaf. What's going on?"

"Nothing. It, uh, it just tickles. So, what'd you think about Ranger Burns coming by?"

"Just doing her job," he says, not looking up.

"Uh-huh." I swallow over a bone-dry lump in my throat. "I'd really like to see some of that jasper. Where do you think it would be? Those archaeologists must know where to find it."

"Well, let's see." He walks to his bookshelves and returns with a thin booklet. "If memory serves me, jasper's mostly found in the Tecovas Formation. Read somewhere that most of it's found up on the rim or at the heads of tributary canyons. Sometimes on the older, alluvial terraces along the canyon floor."

"Alluvial . . . ?"

"Loose rock or soil that's been eroded or that water's redistributed. Dried-up creeks . . . waterways that run off the rim."

"Like near the Lighthouse?"

"That and a hundred other places."

Flipping through pages, I find pictures of the four geological formation layers in Palo Duro Canyon and of rocks, arrowheads and spear points. "Maybe I'll just keep this book awhile."

Dad nods, looking pleased. "Glad to see you expanding your horizons beyond shopping malls."

"Yeah, rocks are great," I mumble. "Totally . . . great."

Why does lying make your shoulders feel so heavy?

CASSIE'S DETECTIVE JOURNAL: Entry #4

<u>Suspicious Behavior</u>

1. Dad and X are in cahoots about something. That much is obvious.
2. Warden Winnie's been making curious comments about Dad since I arrived.

<u>Clues</u>

1. Dad keeps his desk locked up.
2. Warden Winnie thinks the stolen artifacts are still in the canyon.
3. Warden Winnie has a special interest in the Mesquite campground . . . and Dad.

<u>Conclusion</u>

Warden Winnie suspects Dad of being the artifact thief.

CHAPTER TWENTY-SIX

"What trail today?" Dad asks. It's Sunday morning and he's going to take Bobby Ray and me to our hike.

"The Lighthouse," I say quickly.

Bobby Ray groans. "What is it with you and the Lighthouse? We still have one trail left on *our* list, remember? The Rojo Grande."

"I *know.*"

"Rojo Grande it is," Dad says. "Load your packs in the back end. I'll be out in a minute."

"I'll go get Héctor," I tell Bobby Ray on the way to the truck.

"He's not coming," he says.

"Why?"

"'Cause they go to church on Sundays."

"But that means he'll miss *two* of his hikes."

"Prob'ly not a big deal. He's going with us to headquarters tomorrow. If you're worried about it, you can check with Warden Winnie."

That's not what I'm worried about. I need to squeeze more information out of Héctor.

Bobby Ray and I finish up the Rojo Grande Trail fast.

Dad grills chicken breasts for dinner, to go with spinach salad. Because it's Sunday, he's taken over cooking supper.

"Why so quiet, Cassie? Boots still bothering you? Blisters flaring up?"

"No. Just thinking."

He takes the meat off the grill and sets it on the opposite end of the picnic table from Ti, whose leash is fastened to a table leg. Ti lifts his nose, sniffing the aroma of chicken. I pinch off a piece and feed it to him.

"He's getting pretty spoiled with you here," Dad says. "Be hard on him when you leave."

"Maybe Héctor could keep him company. You know, some of the time."

"Looks like they'll be staying here. I'll be heading on down the road all by my lonesome."

"No, you won't." I grin, but my heart's not in it. "You'll have Ti."

"Yep," he says, nodding. "I've got Ti."

"Um, where are the Garcías going to live?"

"They'll be leaving their camper here."

"But where will they go to school?"

"In that town where we shop. A school bus will pick them up out on the road."

"Oh, that's good. There's a college in town, too."

"So there is." He looks at me. "Believe Glinda's folks teach there. Bobby Ray's dad from time to time. Hear he might be applying for a full-time position."

"Oh, yeah?" I sit up straight. "Wouldn't it be great if you could stay here, too?"

"No can do," he says, glancing at the canyon walls. "The wider world calls."

That night while Dad's out taking a shower, I hear a familiar *clink*.

Ears alert, Ti turns his head in the direction of the red toolbox.

"I'll be right back," I whisper.

Slipping out the door, I walk behind the camper so that I'm hidden from view. When I reach the front end, I open the toolbox and feel inside.

It's there . . . an envelope.

I walk to the back of the Winnebago where I'm hidden again. My hands tremble as I open the envelope and pull out the contents.

"Wha—What's this . . . ?"

I fumble over the envelope, patting it for small, sharp objects.

"But I don't understand," I murmur into the darkness.

Worried that Dad will be returning soon, I replace the contents of the envelope and return it to the toolbox.

Inside the camper, I sink down next to Ti. "Just a bunch of papers, no arrowheads. What does it mean, Ti? Why would papers be kept secret?"

Ti flexes his paws on the journal.

"There's nothing to write in it," I tell him. "Same old suspicions. No new clues. At least, none that make sense. What do I do now?"

Only one thing left, I think. Héctor's my only hope.

CHAPTER TWENTY-SEVEN

Monday starts out with a surprise. Glinda has a new haircut. A pixie.

"You look like Tinker Bell," Bobby Ray says. "You know, in *Peter Pan*."

"*Swell,*" Glinda groans. "The littlest shrimp *ever.*" Slumping, she buries her face in folded arms.

"No," Bobby Ray says. "I like it. I like it a *lot*."

"You do?"

"I like it, too." I grin at her.

"*Sí,*" Héctor says. "*Bonita*—pretty."

X nods, smiling.

"*Oh.*" Straightening her shoulders, Glinda smiles all around.

Headquarters is jumping with kids signed up for the Junior Naturalist Program. And sure enough, Héctor can't go with Bobby Ray and me.

"It's because he missed two of the trails, isn't it?" I give Bobby Ray a so-there look. Eyebrows raised, chin tucked.

"Nope," Ranger Burns says. "His vaccination site is inflamed, so I'm keeping him here until it's better. We'll see how it's doing on Wednesday."

Wednesday? But I need to question him *now*.

"I didn't want to get a shot, Cassie," Héctor says. "But Papá made me."

"It's okay. I had to get vaccinated for school, too."

Four really young kids are assigned to Bobby Ray and me, which means they need a lot of help with their study guides. Later, Ranger Burns drives us to the Rojo Grande Trail.

The hike is uneventful, to the point that I'm bored. They see four lizards, one horned, and one rabbit, and take three potty breaks. I even have to give one little hiker a piggyback ride back to the trailhead.

"Good to see you're taking your job so seriously," Ranger Burns tells us on the drive back to the ranger station. "Bobby Ray, drink some water while you're waiting for X and Glinda to get back. You look like you're about to burst into flames."

"Saw a bobcat today," Glinda announces when they arrive.

"Oh, yeah?" My ears perk up. "How big was it?"

"*Mmm*, so-so." She and X sit down under the tree with us and break out water bottles.

"Aw, heck, we never see anything," Bobby Ray complains. "There's not as much wildlife on the short trails. They're too close to the main road and attractions." He looks at me. "We *do* need to hike the longer trails."

He's right, but I have other reasons for wanting to hike the longer trails. One trail in particular.

* * *

We have four students again on Tuesday. Bobby Ray and I take charge of two each, a boy and a girl. Near the turnaround, the boy points to a big rock next to the trail. "Look, Cassie. Someone dropped a rope. I'll go get it."

"*Wait,* Nathan—" The rope is really a rattlesnake, coiled up next to the rock. "Take my hand, we're going to back up now. Real slow, okay?"

"Why?"

"Just do it, then we'll talk."

Out of the snake's striking distance, I take his hand. Ramona, the other little hiker, takes hold of my other one. My knees so shaky I can't stand, I kneel on the trail between them.

"Ropes don't rattle their tails at you, Nathan. That's a rattlesnake's way of talking to you."

"What's it saying?"

"That it doesn't want you to come any closer."

I take out my guide and show them the picture of a rattlesnake. Bobby Ray and his two hikers come back to see why we've stopped. They stare at the snake, their mouths open.

"You did real good, Cassie," Bobby Ray says. "You didn't lose your cool like a lot of girls would've."

Sinking down on a rock, I thank my lucky stars that Bobby Ray wasn't around to see how bad my knees were shaking.

On Wednesday morning, Héctor's arm isn't as red or puffy looking.

"I bet Warden Winnie lets me go today," he says on the drive to headquarters.

Finally, I get to find out what the secret is.

I'm shocked when we walk inside headquarters. Eleven have signed up for the Junior Naturalist Program, and seven are assigned to our team.

How am I going to get Héctor alone so I can question him?

We take our group hiking on Paseo del Rio Trail. About midway, a seven-year-old boy has an emergency. He needs to do number two and there's no restroom nearby.

"You have to take him, Bobby Ray," I say. "He's too little to go alone."

"Why can't you take him?"

"'Cause he's a boy."

His shoulders slump. "Yeah, okay."

"There's a deer trail over there," Héctor says, pointing at a worn track through the brush. "X makes me take one of those when I need to go."

Dropping his backpack on a rock, Bobby Ray pulls TP and his garden trowel from his pack.

"Wait up." I pause a second, mind racing. "Take *all* of them. They need to learn how to dig a hole, too. You know, one that's not near an ant bed or a snake."

"All of them? Why me?"

"'Cause you make a lot of poop," Héctor says, grinning.

"*That's* my claim to fame?" Bobby Ray snaps.

The little boy grabs his sleeve. "I really gotta go—"

"Okay, *okay,*" Bobby Ray sighs. "I guess the rest of you can come, too." He leads them down the deer trail.

"Behind that big clump of sagebrush down there," I call to him. "Not too close to the main path."

"Yeah"—Héctor pinches his fingers on his nose like a clothespin—"*way* down there."

"Let's sit over here." I lead Héctor to a rock outcropping. Sitting down, I lean close so I can look at him at eye level.

"Look, Héctor, I know the secret. See, I found the envelope X left the other night."

"You *know*?" Héctor's eyes look panicky.

"Know what?" I ask.

"About the schoolwork. That X got behind 'cause he didn't go to regular school right away when we moved here in the spring. He missed a few months."

"Wait a minute." I sit up straight. "He and my dad are passing *schoolwork* back and forth? Are you saying my dad's tutoring him?"

"No, he is homeschooling us. My *papá* is not so good reading English words."

I breathe a huge sigh of relief. Dad's not the thief—and he's not an accomplice, either.

"But . . . why do they hide X's homework in those envelopes?"

"X doesn't want anyone to know. You won't tell him I told you, will you? He'll be mad."

"But that's not a bad secret, Héctor." I feel proud that Dad is helping X catch up.

"Yeah, but X says the others will think he's stupid."

Things start to make sense. X's anger when Bobby Ray talked about being smart. The reason he reads so many books. The reason he makes Héctor read all the time.

"He's not stupid," I tell Héctor. "And you're not, either. I mean, just think about it. You moved to a strange place where people speak a different language. That would make everything harder. I'd *never* want to do something like that."

"You mean it?"

"Cross my heart." Knowing the truth, a part of me feels good. The other part feels disappointed.

"What is it, Cassie? You don't look so happy."

"No, I'm happy." I smile at him. "It's just . . . well, I've been looking for something else and thought I'd found it."

"What are you looking for?"

"The missing points."

He looks at me, his face blank.

I pull the book Dad gave me from my pack. "Things that look like this."

"Oh," he says, looking at the pictures of arrowheads and spear points. "I've got some of those."

"You do? Like the ones in these pictures?"

"Three of them."

Three?

"Where—Where'd you get them?"

"I found them. What's wrong, Cassie?"

"*Shh.*" I look off trail to where Bobby Ray is returning with the others. "We'll talk about it later."

"Don't step on plants and stuff," Bobby Ray scolds, trying to herd the returning hikers together. "You're not supposed to damage things." When they reach us, he says, "Everyone take a break. You got water, drink it. You got a snack, eat it."

Dropping down next to me, Bobby Ray pulls a bag of cookies from his pack. "Have to wait for that kid to finish up. I left my trowel so he can cover the hole." He stuffs a cookie in his mouth. "I draw the line there. They can cover up their own poop."

I hand my granola bar to Héctor.

"You don't want it?" he says.

"No, I'm not hungry."

"What's wrong?" Bobby Ray looks me. "You getting sunstroke?"

"No," I say, taking a drink of water. "More like a brain freeze."

CASSIE'S DETECTIVE JOURNAL: Entry #5

Suspicious Behavior (and suspicions)

1. First, it turns out that all my other suspicions were wrong. X isn't a thief. Dad, either. Or Héctor. No one's a thief.
2. BUT I suspect Warden Winnie still thinks Dad is, or else she wouldn't be watching him so close.
3. I also suspect Héctor shouldn't tell anyone he took the points, because he could get people in trouble if he did:
   - Héctor said he and his dad and X just moved to the U.S. this spring. Mr. García is probably here on a work permit.
   - Warden Winnie said even moving an artifact is a federal offense in a state or national park. Even if Héctor didn't know he wasn't supposed to take the points, his father is responsible for him. Mr. García might lose his job, or even get sent back to Mexico.
   - That means his wife and daughters wouldn't be getting any more money sent to them,
   - and X and Héctor wouldn't get to go to school here.

Conclusion

I need to help my friends. But how?

CHAPTER TWENTY-EIGHT

On Friday evening, I watch Dad shake gray dust off his clothes. Cement dust. He and Mr. García repaired foundations today.

Dad wipes grime off his face as he walks inside. "New assignment?" he says, looking at the map on the table.

"Not yet, just getting ready. Ranger Burns could be assigning us to different trails soon."

He looks at the map. "The Lighthouse? You've been wanting to do that one for a while."

"Maybe. But I didn't know it was so big and twisty."

"Lots of loops, all right. Could spend a week just hiking that trail alone."

A week . . . ?

"Think I'll shower before we eat." He puts clean clothes in a tote bag and leaves.

I go back to studying the Lighthouse Trail. And all its loops.

* * *

"These are pretty good," Dad says as we eat supper.

I made pocket pizzas for supper. Pita bread, spaghetti sauce, pepperoni slices and grated cheese in foil packets.

"They're easy to make. Pearl said if we didn't have pepperoni, I could use weenies. You can get creative with recipes, she says."

"You have my permission to get creative any time you want," he says, chuckling.

I push my food around my plate, forking out chunks of cheese for Ti, who's on his leash. He's started joining us for supper at night.

"Pretty quiet tonight." Dad looks at me across the picnic table. "And you're eating like a bird. What's up?"

"Just tired, I guess." Hearing laughter, I look across the campground. X and his gang are already gathering at their spot. Stoking up a fire. Popping tops on soda cans. Laughing. I recognize Bobby Ray from his profile. Glinda from her size. X from his long hair. Héctor isn't in sight.

"Has been a busy week, hasn't it?" Dad says.

If he only knew.

"Lots of kids sign up for the naturalist training?" he asks, taking another pita pocket.

"Yeah—every day."

"*Hmm.* I'm surprised you're not hungrier, hard as you've been working."

I lost my appetite on Wednesday. I haven't talked with Héctor about his arrowheads since then. I can't think of them as the stolen points anymore. Just as missing.

* * *

After we finish dinner and the dishes, I put graham crackers, chocolate bars and marshmallows in a paper sack.

"Where you going?" Dad looks at me as I open the screen door.

Guilt claws at my insides as I utter the lie. "Thought I'd go see what the other kids are up to."

"About time," he says, smiling. "Have fun."

Fun?

CHAPTER TWENTY-NINE

I peer through the screen as I knock on the Garcías' front door. Héctor's sitting at their table with an open book in his hands, his father across from him. They look up at me.

"Um, hi, Mr. García. I came to pick up Héctor." I hold up the paper bag. "We're going to make s'mores."

Héctor stares at me, eyes wide with surprise.

Mr. García smiles. "You go, *m'ijo.* You work hard."

"Okay." Héctor follows me into the yard. "Want me to get some matches to make a fire?"

"No." I look toward the glowing fire pit where the others are sitting. "Let's join the others."

"But X won't like me going over there," Héctor says, dragging his feet.

"Yeah, well, tonight you're allowed. But let's talk first." I rub the ache between my eyes, then look at him. "I need to see those arrowheads you found, Héctor."

His face falls. "Why?"

"We need to take them back where you found them."

"No—they're mine. Finders keepers."

"But they don't belong to you. You know the rules here. You're not supposed to pick up things."

His lower lip juts out. "I never get to keep anything. Fish. *Nopales*. Potato chips."

"I know, but it's what we have to do. Now, where are they?"

Sighing, he pulls a small, crumpled brown bag from one of the storage tubs under the table.

Peeking inside, I see two small arrowheads and a longer one. The missing Plano points.

"If you tell X," he says, "he'll be mad at me."

"I'll explain it to him." Folding the brown bag into a small packet, I stuff it in my pocket. "They know the trails better than I do. We need their help."

"X doesn't listen too good, Cassie," Héctor says as we resume walking toward the others. "He'll be *real* mad."

"Prob'ly," I sigh. "But I can't do this alone."

"What? What're you going to do?"

"Well, see, I have a plan."

X, Bobby Ray and Glinda are surprised when Héctor and I walk up. Fortunately, no one else has joined them.

"What are you doing here, Héctor?" X says. "You're supposed to be reading to Papá."

"Your dad said it was okay," I tell him. "I told him we were making s'mores." I set the sack containing the ingredients on the table.

"*Sweet.*" Bobby Ray begins forking marshmallows onto straightened clothes hangers.

"But the s'mores were just a diversion." I pull Héctor forward. "See, we've got a problem, a *serious* problem."

"*Uh-oh.*" Glinda looks at Bobby Ray. "C'mon, I think that's our cue to beat it."

"No, stay—*please.*" Sinking onto a log next to the fire pit, I pull Héctor down next to me. "It's going to take all of us to fix this."

"That was *stupid*, Héctor." X glares at his little brother, fists knotted. "How could you do something so *stupid*?"

"It was an accident," Héctor says. "I didn't know 'bout not pickin' up stuff then."

"But where was I?" X says. "I would've stopped you."

"It was one of the times I had to go. 'Member, you always made me go off the trail?"

"Why didn't you tell me about them? Why didn't you show me the things you took?"

"'Cause you never let me keep anything," Héctor says.

X holds his head, groaning.

"Well now," Bobby Ray says, staring between the brothers. "How 'bout them apples?"

"Why do you say that?" Glinda snaps. "What's it even mean, anyway?"

"I dunno." Bobby Ray shrugs. "My grandpa says it all the time and people just nod like they understand."

Glinda grins at him. "Well, from now on, would you just say what *you're* thinking?"

Bobby Ray blinks. "But see, that's just it. I don't know what to think."

I can't help but laugh, which makes everyone look at me like I've gone loony. "I think you just figured out what it means, Bobby Ray."

"Oh . . . yeah." He takes a deep breath. "Okay, here's

what I'm thinking. Now that we know what really happened, what the heck are we supposed do about it? I mean, this is *serious* stuff. You remember what Warden Winnie said? People go to jail for this kind of thing."

"Jail?" Héctor's eyes are round as donuts. "Don't let them tell on me, Cassie. I don't want to go to jail."

"No one's telling on you, Héctor." I wrap an arm around his shoulders. "We're going to fix it."

Everyone looks at me. Waiting.

"Do you have sunstroke?" Glinda says after I tell them my plan. "What do you mean, 'We'll just take them back'?"

"All we need to do is find this archaeological dig. Héctor remembers gathering some *nopales* on cactus and seeing the Lighthouse. So it has to be on one of the trails that lead to it. You and X know the trails best, and Bobby Ray knows all about plants. And I learned that the Indians used jasper to make their points, so the dig's probably near a creek bed. Someplace where water has run off, that's where jasper's found." I pause, looking at their stunned faces. "We can do this. Together we can do this."

"Wow," Bobby Ray says, looking impressed. "That's good deduction."

Glinda looks at me like I'm crazy. "Do you know how many trails you're talking about? In addition to the loops, the main trail connects with the Givens Trail and the Little Fox Canyon Trail and—"

"We get it—we get it," Bobby Ray groans.

"See, it might not be that complicated. I checked the map and only one creek runs alongside the trail. And we can search without raising suspicions because we're guides." I look around the fire pit at their shadowy faces.

The flickering of the campfire makes it hard to tell what they're thinking.

"You're right." Glinda nods. "No one would suspect us because we're supposed to be there."

"Yeah, we have the perfect alibi for snooping around," Bobby Ray says, grinning. "It could work."

Slowly, Glinda grins, too. "Yeah, it *really* could."

"I can't let you do this," X says. He starts pacing, kicking up fine dust like a cloud.

"Why?" Glinda says.

"'Cause he thinks it would be like a handout," I say, looking at X.

"But it's not," Glinda says. "Just think, we'll be detectives after all!"

"Yeah, crime busters," Bobby Ray says.

"Well, there really isn't a crime," I say. "It was just a mistake."

"Yeah, a mistake," Héctor echoes.

Bobby nods slowly. "Okay, then we'll be crime *stoppers.* And we'll call ourselves the U-Turn Crime Stoppers Gang."

"U-turn . . . ?" Glinda raises her eyebrows.

"Yeah. You know, like when you turn around and go back the way you came. We'll be crime stoppers that undo the crime!"

"I like it," she says. "It's catchy."

"Not *gang,*" I say. "Gangs do bad things."

"Oh, okay," Bobby Ray says. "Um, how 'bout *bunch*? The U-Turn Crime Stoppers Bunch."

"That makes us sound like a bunch of grapes," Glinda says, drumming her fingers on the table. "Society," she says slowly. "The U-Turn Crime Stoppers Society, that's what we'll call ourselves."

"Cool," Bobby Ray says.

X shakes his head. "No way. I can't let you risk getting in trouble."

"Please, X," Héctor pleads.

"I was responsible for you," X says, "so *I'll* fix it. Where'd you hide them? I'll take them back."

"No fair," Glinda says. "You can't leave us out. It's the first thing this summer that hasn't been boring."

"I vote for sticking together," says Bobby Ray. "All for one and one for all, just like the musketeers."

Glinda looks at me. "What do you think, Cassie?"

"I think . . ." I feel my heart start to throb. "I think my mom wanted me to have an adventure this summer." I look at X. "And I've got the points *and* a perfect hiding place until we can return them. Someplace no one would ever look."

"Okay, that's taken care of," Glinda says. "We need to lay the groundwork carefully. Like coming up with a reason for all of us to be dropped off at the Lighthouse trailhead. That way, after Warden Winnie leaves, Héctor can go with X and me to find where he left the trail, instead of Cassie and Bobby Ray."

X groans into his hands again.

"What do you say, X?" Bobby Ray asks. "You with us?"

"Okay, *okay.*" X looks around the campfire at us. "But when it comes to putting them back at the dig site, Héctor and I'll do it. No one else. That way if we get caught, the rest of you will be in the clear."

"Agreed," Bobby Ray says. Glinda and I nod.

"We have to go on like normal," Glinda says. "You know, so we don't alert Warden Winnie to what we're up to." Her smile rivals the Cheshire Cat's. "Finally, something *fun* to do."

That word again.

As I return to the Winnebago, I see Dad sitting at Charlie and Pearl's campfire. Hurrying inside, I remove the paper bag with the points from my pocket.

Nudging Ti aside, I look at how the bound pages in the journal slip into the cover's front and back flaps. Quickly, I examine the three points. The two small ones look like arrowheads, the third's a little longer. And all are thin enough to slide under the back flap.

Returning the journal to the window ledge, I whisper, "Guard these with your life, Ti."

He sniffs the journal's new smells. As Dad's footsteps crunch across the driveway, Ti curls up on it again.

Perfect. No one would ever bother a blind cat.

CHAPTER THIRTY

Going on like normal is hard when you know secrets. So we make some rules.

U-Turn Crime Stoppers Society Rules

1. Don't do anything dopey around Warden Winnie—especially giggling and whispering because that would make her suspicious.
2. Act natural around our parents and other adults so they'll ignore us.

Unfortunately, the rules don't seem to work.

Dad waves at Héctor and X on the way to town on Saturday. They turn their backs on us.

"What's up with them?" Dad asks, frowning. "That's not like them."

Mumbling "Dunno," I stare out the window.

Glinda becomes a campground gymnast when we

pass her, jumping around like a squirrel that's forgotten where it hid its acorns. Bobby Ray tries to hide behind a yucca plant—a *spiky* yucca plant. We hear him yelling "*Ouch-ouch-ouch!*" all the way out of the Mesquite.

So much for acting normal, I think.

"We'll call your mom first," Dad says.

"Who?"

"Your mom." He glances at me. "This is the day we're supposed to call her."

"Oh, yeah. I forgot."

"You forgot?" He looks at me like an alien has crawled inside my skin.

"Yeah, everything's good, Mom. I'm, uh, I'm keeping real busy. You know, being a junior guide and learning how to cook on a campfire." I hear a pause on the line.

"You are being careful, aren't you, Cassie? Campfires can get out of control. And there are snakes there. Dangerous animals, too."

"I'm being real careful."

"That's a relief." She sighs loudly. "Now, I'm afraid I'm still working on your coming to Europe, but I should know something in another week or so."

Perfect. Time for us to fix Héctor's problem.

I look at Dad. "Can we call again in a week or two? She's working on some things."

"Maybe she can leave me a message, let us know when it's a good time."

I pass the message on to Mom.

"Yes, that makes sense. Well then, must go. I'm flying to Hamburg tonight. Love you, Cassie."

"Me, too, Mom."

Dad stares at the road on the drive to town. Lips zipped shut.

"She, uh, she doesn't know anything yet," I volunteer.

"These things take time," he says. "You make a grocery list?"

"Not yet." I pull index cards from my pack. "Pearl copied off more recipes for me to try. Foil Fries. Pizza Crisp. Brown Bears."

"What's a Brown Bear?" he asks.

I study the recipe card. "They're made with cinnamon, sugar, melted butter and canned biscuits."

"Sounds like sticky buns," he says. "And here I was hoping I'd be cutting into a big bear steak tonight."

"I'll write up a grocery list."

"Put an extra quart of milk on it," he says, grinning. "Tomato soup would taste a *little* better if you'd thin it with milk instead of water."

I make a face at him.

"Want to call your friends later?" he says.

I stare at the road for a minute, then say, "Nah, that's okay."

CHAPTER THIRTY-ONE

The U-Turn Crime Stoppers Society is in the back of Dad's pickup, heading for the ranger station.

"Today we have to convince Warden Winnie to let Bobby Ray and me hike the Lighthouse Trail."

"Why wouldn't she?" Bobby Ray says. "It's been two weeks now. Your blisters are healed up."

Glinda rolls her eyes at him.

"What?" he says.

"Cassie's not the problem," X says, laughing. "You look like you're about to explode when you get back from the *short* trails."

"Nuh-uh . . ." Bobby Ray looks at me. "Do I?"

"Well, you do get pretty red in the face."

"I've always been sensitive to the sun." He looks at his arm. "See, freckles everywhere. But I have lots of stamina. And I've been to the Lighthouse already. Last year when we came."

"Ranger Burns made us a deal," Glinda says, blinking

slowly. "She said she'd change up the teams later, give us new trails."

"So it's time to hold her to the deal?" I ask.

Glinda nods, grinning.

"High fives!" Bobby Ray yells quickly.

The sound of palms slapping fills the back of the pickup.

"Why the Lighthouse Trail?" Ranger Burns says when I bring it up.

"'Cause it's the most famous landmark in the canyon." I let my shoulders droop, turn the corners of my mouth down. "And I'm the only junior guide who hasn't seen it yet. Bobby Ray's even hiked there."

"Yeah," Bobby Ray says. "You should let her do it. I mean, the loops don't look that long. Bet they're not much longer than what we've been doing. That way, she'd get a good look at the park's most famous landmark."

"Right," Glinda says. "He and Cassie can take the loops and X and I can do the main trail."

"Well . . ." Ranger Burns looks at me, forehead wrinkled. "If you think you're ready."

"Oh, *more* than ready," I say, bobbing my head.

That night around the campfire, we develop our strategy. Bobby Ray and I will cover the Lighthouse loops one at a time. X and Glinda will investigate segments of the main Lighthouse Trail.

"Take field glasses," Glinda says.

"What're we looking for . . . exactly?" Bobby Ray asks. "I've never seen an archaeology dig."

"*Digging.*" X snickers. "Ground that's been disturbed. Maybe stakes and strings marking off boundaries."

"Héctor's the one who would recognize it first," Glinda says.

"But it's too far," Héctor says. "I wanna stay with Cassie."

"*Flojo,*" X snaps, glaring at him.

"Why do you always talk so ratty to him?" I don't know what *flojo* means, but the way X says it, it can't be good.

X scowls at me. "*You* wouldn't understand."

The next time Héctor and I are alone, I ask, "What did X mean when he said I wouldn't understand?"

Héctor ducks his chin. "We need to get good jobs to help Papá. We can't be *flojo*. Lazy."

"Is that what he meant on that first day at the picnic table? You know, when he told you to speak English?"

"*Burro,*" he whispers. "He called me *burro*. It means donkey, stupid like a donkey. We need to speak good English so we get rich. You know, like you."

"Rich? I'm not rich."

"*Sí*. You are rich."

"So *that's* why X doesn't like me?"

"No." He stares at his feet. "You wouldn't talk to him. He thinks you are *una fresa*, a stuck-up girl."

"Oh. Well, see, it was those tattoos."

"You don't like them?"

"Where I live, tough kids have tattoos like that. Kids in gangs that do bad things."

"Not X, he would never do that. He wants to be smart like Lucas. You know, be his own *jefe*."

"What's that?"

"Boss. He wants to be boss like Lucas." Héctor's head hangs. "I messed things up bad."

"Me, too, Héctor," I sigh. "Me, too."

CHAPTER THIRTY-TWO

Ranger Burns officially assigns us our new routes on the Lighthouse Trail on Tuesday. X and Glinda get the main trail, of course, and Bobby Ray and me, the loops. Héctor is to go with Bobby Ray and me.

"What do we do?" Bobby Ray moans. We're standing outside headquarters waiting for Ranger Burns to come out. "Héctor *has* to go with the A-team."

"I *know,*" I whisper. "It'll all work out."

"*Shh,*" Glinda says. "Here she comes."

"Why are you dillydallying?" Ranger Burns bellows. "Load up. You think I've got all day?"

When we arrive at the Lighthouse Trail, she asks if we brought plenty of food and water. "Because this one's longer, you'll be eating on the trail." She looks at Bobby Ray. "Restroom breaks, too. So make sure you're prepared."

"I got TP," he says. "A brand-new roll."

She nods. "The student load is light today. Only six students, split evenly between you. I need to get some reports out, but two other rangers on patrol will be checking on you. You good with that?"

Stealing glances at each other, we try not to grin.

"Be smart," Ranger Burns cautions us. "Don't go maverick on me."

We watch as her car disappears in a cloud of rust-colored dust.

"Maverick?" I look around at the others.

"Rad," Bobby Ray says. "She doesn't want us to do anything radical."

"Too late," Glinda says as we start off. "Here's the new plan. Héctor's going with X and me." She pulls binoculars from her backpack. "Focus on dry stream beds. Got it?"

"Divide and conquer!" Bobby Ray yells, tearing down our assigned loop.

On Friday, Glinda, X and Héctor find the place where he veered off the Lighthouse Trail. Héctor recognizes it because of a prickly pear cactus that's missing a lot of its leaves. He confesses to gathering *nopales* for his father and hiding them in his day pack.

"Now what?" Glinda asks that night. "When do we take the points back?"

We're sitting at the fire pit, roasting marshmallows. A couple of the other kids staying at the Mesquite tried to join us, but X sent them packing. Which meant we had to add a new item to the U-Turn Crime Stoppers Society Rules.

> No new members allowed under any circumstances because they might have loose lips.

"Yeah, when?" Bobby Ray says. "We can't do it during the week when the kids in the Naturalist Program are with us."

"I've been thinking about it," X says. "I need to do this alone because Héctor would just slow me down."

"But Héctor *has* to be there," I insist. "The points have to be put back exactly where he found them."

"That's stupid. No one will notice if I get it wrong."

"*Hello.*" Bobby Ray snorts. "What planet did you just beam down from? You really think Warden Winnie is *that* dumb?"

"Yeah," Glinda says. "Besides, those archaeologists take pictures. Cassie's right, it has to be exact."

"Well then, that means we do it on a Sunday," X says, sighing. "After lunch on Sunday is the only time that would work." He looks at me. "It's, uh, it's time to go get the points, Cassie. So I can hide them in my backpack."

"Oh, no you don't." I grin at him. "I'm not *that* dumb, either. I'll bring them with me Sunday afternoon. I'm finishing this adventure!"

CHAPTER THIRTY-THREE

"You seem distracted," Dad says. He's driving us to the top of the canyon where we can get good cell phone reception. Mom left a message for us to call her on Saturday at the regular time.

"I, uh, I didn't sleep so well last night."

"Oh? Ti seemed restless, too."

He's right. Ti was all over the place before we left, ricocheting from one of his window shelves to another. I even looked outside to see if a raccoon was trying to get into the trash barrel. There wasn't anything in sight.

"Must be something in the air." Dad glances toward the horizon. "Chance of rain, maybe that's it." He looks at me. "Didn't I tell you Ti was psychic?"

I force a grin, but inside, I'm not smiling. I'm wondering if Ti was telling me he knew what we were about to do. If maybe he was sending me a message.

What? I wonder. What was he trying to tell me?

* * *

“I have exciting news, Cassie,” Mom says.

“You did it—you fixed it so I could come to Europe, didn’t you? When? When do I come? For how long? Do I leave from here? Can Dad take me to the airport?”

“Slow down.” She sounds like she’s a million miles away. “It’s a little more complicated than that. Let me talk to your father first.”

“She wants to talk to you.” I hand Dad the phone. “She says it’s complicated.”

Dad sighs when he takes the phone. He listens mostly, then says, “I understand.” He hands the phone back without looking at me.

“What is it, Dad?”

“I’ll let your mother tell you. I’ll just step outside the truck so you two can talk.”

“Two years! But Mom . . .”

I listen as Mom talks about the two-year assignment she’s gotten in Europe.

“It’s a once-in-a-lifetime opportunity, Cassie. And I’ve found a good boarding school for you. Because I’ll be traveling a lot, that would be best. I know you hate leaving your friends in Austin, but just think of the new friends you’ll make.”

That’s it, I think. That’s what Ti was warning me about. My head spinning, I look for Dad. Tapping on the windshield, I wave him back inside the truck.

“What is it?” His forehead wrinkles.

“Cassie . . . Cassie . . . Are you still on the line?”

“Mom’s enrolling me in a boarding school. Did you know that?”

"She . . . mentioned it."

"Does that mean I have to live at the school all the time?"

"As I understand it, students go home for long weekends and holidays."

"Two years is a long time."

"It's . . it's a wonderful educational opportunity. Few kids your age get the chance."

"Cassie—do we still have a connection?"

"But Dad, what if I don't want to go?"

"*What?*" says Mom's voice in my ear. Dad takes the phone from me. "We'll call you back, Rebecca. Give us a few minutes."

Dad thought I needed more time to think about it, but it only took me a split second to make up my mind.

"What do you mean you don't want to come, Cassie?" Mom said. "You have to come—you have no choice. I've already sublet the apartment in Austin."

"I'll stay here with Dad. His camper's real nice. It has everything you could possibly need."

Dad touches my sleeve. "I didn't think you liked the trailer."

"I didn't," I whisper. "At first."

"And where would you go to school?" Mom asks. "He moves all over the place."

"He can homeschool me." I glance at Dad. "Just like he's been doing with some of the other kids."

Dad raises his eyebrows at me.

"Héctor told me," I whisper, "but I promised I wouldn't let X know."

"He's been homeschooling others?" Mom says. "No, Cassie. You have to live with me."

"No, I don't, Mom. You and Dad share custody, remember? It's just I've been staying with you mostly. It's his turn now."

Dad takes the phone again. "If you think about it, Rebecca, it makes sense. You can focus on your new job and Cassie would be in good hands, far better than leaving her with strangers. Besides"—he hesitates, rubbing his bottom lip—"I have options."

Options? I look at Dad, but he's not through talking to Mom.

"You'll be flying back to Austin from time to time, so you can see Cassie then. I'll make sure of it." He smiles at me. "Maybe she can fly over there now and then, too. To see castles and museums and things like that."

Grinning, I shake my head up and down.

He pauses, listening. "All right, then. I'll give her the news."

"You think Mom will be okay?" We're driving back to the Mesquite.

"She's very resilient," Dad says. "And smart. She could see that this was a good decision. You'll probably see more of her this way than if you moved to Germany." He glances at me. "One thing to get straight right now. I expect you to follow *all* the house rules."

"There's more?"

"Yep, and you're not going to like some of them."

"Like, which ones?"

He grins. "Oh, you'll know when you run into them."

"Come on, give me a hint?"

He pauses, thinking. "Well, for starters, if I homeschool you, you'll be just another student. Don't expect special treatment."

"Yeah, sure. That's okay."

He glances my way again, not smiling. "Cassie, I've noticed you and X don't get along, and I think you're the one who's been driving that situation. In my house, no one's any better than anyone else. Understand?"

"I do, Dad—totally." I look at him. "I know I've acted like a . . . *una fresa.* A snobby girl."

He grins at me. "Héctor teach you that?"

I nod.

"Okay," he continues, "I also want to see you challenge yourself more with your cooking. Try some of Pearl's harder recipes."

"Got it. No more tomato soup thinned with water."

He smiles again. "And from here on out, you strip your own bed, run the vacuum at least once a week and . . ." He looks at me. "Clean Ti's litter box every day."

"*Every* day?"

"Every day," he repeats. "I keep a covered pail under the Winnebago, and once a week, it gets carried to the Dumpster there at the Mesquite."

I answer with a sigh and a nod.

"And one more thing."

I tense up, waiting.

"I want to see you step outside your comfort zone."

I stare at him. "Dad, I don't even know what that means."

He looks at me directly. "It means you're afraid of your shadow. Life's too short, can't play it safe all the time."

He thinks I'm a wimp. What would he do if he knew what the U-Turn Society was planning—and whose idea it was?

He grins at me. "I'll tell you the rest of the rules as I think of them."

I just groan.

CHAPTER THIRTY-FOUR

"What time should I pick you up?" Dad is driving the others and me to the Lighthouse trailhead in a few minutes. We've gathered in our living room.

"Oh, we didn't talk about that." I look toward X and Glinda. They're the ones who know how far we need to go to return the Plano points.

"Five o'clock, Lucas," X says. "Pick us up at the trailhead at five."

"A little late in the day to finish a hike," Dad says, frowning slightly. "But I need to run into town to respond to an e-mail. I'll do that and be back for you at five o'clock."

Respond to an e-mail . . . That means he got a job offer. Where, I wonder.

Dad looks at each of us. "Everyone have plenty of water? Food?"

"I got plenty," Bobby Ray says.

"He always has plenty of everything," Héctor says. "'Specially toilet paper."

Dad laughs. "Well, all right then. Get in the truck. I'll be right out."

The trailhead is busy with hikers, bikers and horseback riders.

"You bring the points?" X whispers. He's walking behind me. Héctor's in front. Glinda's in the lead, with Bobby Ray close behind.

"In my pack—and you're not getting your hands on them till we get there. You'll take off running and leave the rest of us in your dust."

I hear quiet laughter behind me.

Our hiking boots make a loud scuffing sound. The other people on the trail are taking their time. Looking at the cliffs, the marshmallow clouds on the horizon. Listening to birds sing, looking through binoculars at wildlife. But not us. The U-Turn Crime Stoppers Society is on a mission.

"Let's take a break," Bobby Ray wheezes.

We've been walking almost an hour, and Glinda has set a fast pace. For a girl with short legs, she's a speed demon.

"Plenty of time for a break on the way back," she says, tromping ahead.

When we reach a place on the trail that runs alongside a dry creek bed, Glinda hesitates, looking at X.

"Yeah," he says, nodding. "This looks like it."

"Finally," Bobby Ray says, collapsing on a boulder.

X walks up to me, holding out a palm. "Hand 'em over, Warden Cassie."

"*Warden?* I'm nothing like her."

"Oh, yeah?" He raises an eyebrow at me.

I look around cautiously before unzipping a pocket on my backpack, but the stretch of the trail we're on is quiet. Even though I've wrapped the points in tissue to protect them, I handle them carefully.

"Wait," I whisper, looking X in the eyes. "I, uh, I'm sorry I acted like *una fresa*. It was the tattoos. I thought they meant you were in a gang."

"*Una fresa*?" he says, grinning.

I feel my cheeks start to burn. "Héctor's teaching me Spanish."

Glancing at his tattoos, he shrugs. "My friends were doing it. So, you know."

"Yeah," I say, nodding. "I do know."

"Show us," Glinda says, walking up close to us. "Let us see the points, too."

"Wow, five thousand years old." Bobby Ray touches one of the points with a fingertip.

"Yeah, and see how pretty they are." I turn one of the points so it reflects the light.

"Look," Glinda says. "There's patterns in them, like miniature landscapes."

"Okay, c'mon, Héctor." X slips the points into his pocket. "The rest of you keep watch. You need to warn us, screech like a red-tailed hawk. I'll do a meadowlark call when we get back there." He points out a cluster of mesquite. "You answer like another meadowlark when it's all clear."

He and Héctor walk quickly across the dry creek and disappear in thick mesquite and sagebrush.

"Meadowlark," Bobby Ray says, looking at me. "What's its call sound like?"

"You're asking *me*?"

Glinda just rolls her eyes.

Bobby Ray decides to take a water break, accompanied with two granola bars, the diet kind, of course, so Glinda and I end up standing watch.

"You look that way," Glinda says, pointing up the trail. "I'll watch down this way. And keep your field glasses in your hand so people will think we're bird-watching. Whatever you do, don't arouse the suspicions of a park ranger. They'll be on the trails, too."

Birds don't interest me. I focus my binoculars instead on the Lighthouse, which isn't far away. I even spot the trail on the canyon wall that Dad climbed down. As I follow the canyon wall to where we're standing, I see other animal trails leading down from the rim. Dozens of them.

"*Ohmigosh—*" I watch a tawny streak racing up a nearby trail.

"What?" Glinda rushes to my side. "You see a park ranger?"

"No—a bobcat. I saw a bobcat."

Her shoulders sag in relief. "Geez, you scared the pee out of me." She looks up and down the trail. "You notice how empty the trail is?"

No one's in sight, in either direction. "Where'd everybody go?"

"I don't think that's the right question," Glinda says, her forehead wrinkling. "*Why'd* they go is what's worrying me."

"Kind of late in the day," Bobby Ray says, joining us. "Probably headed back to eat supper."

Glinda frowns. "It's not *that* late."

A niggling buzz starts up in my head, like a pesky fly that won't leave me alone. I train my field glasses on the sky. The marshmallow clouds on the horizon look like they've been toasted over a campfire. More black than white.

"Uh-oh, check out those clouds."

"Aw, man," Glinda mutters. "That's not good."

Bobby Ray looks where we're looking. "Oh, *crap*. You bring a rain slicker? I did, I got one." He starts fumbling with his pack.

"Hold up. If they get back here quick, you might not need it." Glinda looks toward the creek bed. "Where *are* they?"

"Yeah." Bobby Ray looks at his watch. "They've been gone a long time."

I check my watch, too. "Dad's supposed to pick us up in an hour. We barely have enough time to get back to the trailhead."

Ten minutes pass. It starts to sprinkle.

"You hear any birds?" I whisper.

Glinda and Bobby Ray swivel their necks, listening.

"The clouds are getting darker, too," Bobby Ray says.

I look toward the horizon, what there is of it. The canyon walls are so close, not much sky shows.

"*Look.*" Glinda points up the creek bed. The sand is turning darker between the rocks. "That's water seeping from upstream. Must be pouring up there."

"We have to go get them." I step into the creek bed. "We won't get across this creek if we don't go now."

We encounter X and Héctor not long after we leave the trail. X is carrying Héctor on his back.

"What took you so long—?" Glinda spots the bloody sock wrapped around Héctor's right leg.

"Did he get snake-bit?" Bobby Ray says. "Oh, geez, did you suck out the blood?"

"Not a snake bite," X says. "Héctor had a hard time finding the exact spots where he found the points. I think the archaeologists had done more digging." He pauses, setting Héctor on a rock. "Then he fell off a boulder and stabbed his leg on a mesquite stump."

Opening his backpack, Bobby Ray pulls out a small first-aid kit. "My mom's a nurse. She makes me carry this everywhere. I never got to use it before."

"Wow," Glinda says, examining the kit. "That's cool."

Bobby Ray looks at Héctor. "This is going to hurt, but I have to do it." Removing the improvised bandage, he pours water over the wound, then sprays it with antiseptic spray.

"Does it hurt, Héctor?" I sit down next to him.

"A little." His face looks pale.

Bobby Ray puts a clean dressing on Héctor's leg and wraps it with an Ace Bandage. "There, all done."

"We need to hurry." X looks in the direction we came from. "That creek will flood."

"Too late," Glinda says. "It's probably impassable already."

Given her size, Glinda wouldn't be able to ford anything too deep. Héctor, either. *Any* of us, for that matter. I remember hearing somewhere that it doesn't take a lot of water to knock someone off their feet.

"Yeah, we can't go back that way." I look at Glinda. "What do we do? Which way do we go?"

"Nowhere—we stay put," Bobby Ray says. "You read that in all the safety bulletins. If you get lost, stay put."

"Yeah," Glinda says. "I bet they've already put the word out on their two-ways. They'll come find us."

"But we *can't* stay here," X says. "They find us here, they'll know we were the ones that took the points and brought them back."

Héctor's eyes well up. "I don't want to go to jail. . . ."

I look at Glinda again. "You said the Lighthouse Trail connected with lots of others. Which one's the closest?"

"I . . . I'm not sure. I never left a trail before. And the brush is so thick." She turns in a slow circle. "I don't know where we are . . . exactly."

No one speaks. The clouds on the horizon get bigger. The sky changes to a greenish gray. The air turns cold.

Bobby Ray looks at us, his eyes huge. "We need to find shelter."

"We go up," I say, looking at the canyon wall where I saw the bobcat. "We climb to the rim. There's an old house up there where we can wait out the storm."

I lead off, jogging toward the canyon wall. "Hurry! We have to make it up before that storm reaches us."

CHAPTER THIRTY-FIVE

The deer trail is steep and slippery. We scramble like goats. Grab hold of roots for handholds. Give each other boosts at steep places. Mutter when something jabs us or we scrape against a rock.

"You okay, Héctor?" He's wedged between X and me. Bookends to make sure he doesn't fall.

"My leg hurts," he grunts.

Thunder rumbles louder, getting closer. The light is fading faster. By the time we clamber onto the rim, the sky is studded with lightning, looking like blinking Christmas lights. Breathless, we stop to rest.

"Okay, Cassie," X says, looking around. "Which way?"

"There's a road. Spread out and look for it."

"Stay in sight of each other," X cautions. He hoists Héctor onto his back and starts off in one direction. The rest of us angle off, too.

"Found it!" Bobby Ray calls out.

We hurry toward the sound of his voice. The sky is

darkening by the second. The bottoms of the clouds have a deep-green cast to them. Suddenly, they open up.

"My slicker . . ." Bobby Ray fumbles with his backpack.

"No time for that," Glinda says. "Just keep going."

"How much farther, Cassie?" Bobby Ray gasps. Water drips off his nose. "It's really getting dark."

"Just stay on the road. I know it leads to that house."

"Wait." X comes to a stop. "The road splits here." He looks at me. "Which way do we go?"

"I . . . I don't remember it splitting. And I can't see a foot in front of me."

"Wait for the lightning," Glinda says. "Look around when it flashes."

As the sky lights up, a ghostly silhouette appears in the distance. A dark square shape that's out of place.

"There—that has to be it."

"Let's take a shortcut," X says, taking the lead. "Follow me."

Bobby Ray lags behind. "But there's things out there. Prickly pear and yucca. Even *snakes.*"

"Just hold your hands out in front of you like feelers," I yell. "That way, you'll find the cactus and yucca. And listen close. If you hear something rattling, stop and walk around it."

"*Ow,*" Glinda moans.

"Did you get bit?" Bobby Ray says.

"No, I ran into a yucca."

"Stay behind me," Bobby Ray says. He stumbles ahead of her. "Here, take my hand, I'll lead you."

With Héctor on his back, X looks like a giant monster. Glinda and Bobby Ray are bobbing black blobs. Tripping over a rock, I feel a cactus thorn puncture my knee. The lightning strikes are coming faster. The thunder is deafening. I struggle to my feet and hurry to catch up with the moving blobs ahead.

The house looks just the same when we reach it. A ghost house surrounded with spiky grass, sagebrush and knobby trees.

"Good, it's boarded up." X sets Héctor on the ground next to me. "No cows or big animals could've gotten in."

I feel Héctor's hand slip into mine.

"Pull those tumbleweeds away," X tells Bobby Ray. "We need to find a door."

"Here it is," Bobby Ray says. The door gives easily when he shoves against it. "*Phew.* It smells like scat. And it's pitch-black."

"Mice and squirrels probably climbed in from the roof," X says. "You're smelling their scat."

I peer inside. Utter darkness. This is what Ti sees, I think. I'm seeing with Ti's eyes.

"At least it's dry and doesn't have thorns," Glinda says, pushing past us.

As the rest of us crowd through the door, hail starts to beat on the old metal roof. The darkness is as thick as tar. Holding out my hands, I realize there are some things you can't feel your way around. Open space . . . open space that could be swarming with things.

My skin starts to crawl. "Spiders—there's probably spiders and scorpions."

"Stay in the middle of the room," X says. "They'll be in the corners most likely, behind old boards."

"We're supposed to stand up all night?" Héctor says. "But my leg hurts."

"We can sit on my slicker." Bobby Ray pulls a crinkly

piece of plastic from his backpack that reflects yellow in the dim light. "Take a corner, spread it out. Sit in a circle with your back to the others. That way, we can lean on each other."

We huddle together. Listen to rain drum on the roof. Watch lightning flash through the boarded-up windows. Shiver.

"That was neat, Bobby Ray." Darkness amplifies Glinda's whisper. "You know, the way you fixed up Héctor . . . *and* the way you cleared trail for me."

"Yeah? You, uh, you want, you can lean on my shoulder."

"Oh . . . okay," Glinda whispers.

I smile into the darkness, then feel sad. "Too bad some of us have to move away soon," I say. "I don't even know where I'll be going."

"Oh, I'm not moving," Bobby Ray says. "My dad got a job, so we're staying here. Dad already found us a house in town."

"No joke?" Glinda says. "That means we'll go to the same school."

"*Sweet,*" Bobby says.

"Us, too," X says. "My dad says it's time he stopped moving around so much, so Héctor and I don't have to change schools all the time."

That means I'm the only one moving away. . . .

No one talks for a while. Then X says, "Thanks, everyone. You know, for looking out for us."

"*Sí,*" Héctor whispers. He leans against my shoulder. "Thanks for breaking the rules."

"Well, sometimes it's okay to break the rules," I tell him. "At least, that's what I think."

"Me, too," Bobby Ray says. "My grandpa says there are two sides to every rule just like there's two sides to every coin. You should *always* break a rule if it's an emergency and you need to help someone, but don't break it if it's not."

"Good grief," Glinda says. "Sometimes your grandpa makes sense."

It gets quiet again, then X says, "Lucas says you're going to live with him now, Cassie. Is it because your *mamá* is moving to Europe?"

"Two years, she's staying two years. Dad's going to homeschool me."

"Wow, that's cool," Bobby Ray says. "I wish my parents would homeschool me, but they're too busy."

"So, homeschooling is a good thing, then?" X says.

"The greatest," Bobby Ray says.

I feel someone fidgeting at my back, then hear X's voice.

"Lucas has been homeschooling me and Héctor. I don't know who will help us after we start at the town school."

"Mystery solved," Glinda snorts. "I thought you were cracked in the head, reading all the time like that."

"You need any help with math, I can help you," Bobby Ray says. "I'm good at math."

"Me, too," Glinda says. "I'm good at English and social studies."

"And I'm good at writing papers. I can help you . . . as long as I'm here," I offer.

"*Gracias,*" X says. "I mean, thanks."

I smile, and though it's pitch-black, I know X is smiling, too.

CHAPTER THIRTY-SIX

The storm lasts a long time, but finally the pounding rain turns to a steady drizzle. We divide what food we have left, and by the time we leave the old house at daybreak, the mesquite and yucca sparkle with dewdrops. The air is scented with juniper and sage warmed in morning sunshine. We feel so good, we don't even complain about the scratches and scrapes we got on the climb up. Then Héctor reminds us of what we're still up against.

"My *papá* will be real worried, Cassie."

"I know. All our folks will be."

"I am going to be *so* grounded," Bobby Ray moans. "No DVDs or games for a month."

"Yeah, and Warden Winnie will probably fire us," Glinda says.

"Where's this road lead, Cassie?" X asks, changing the subject. "Is it how you got here?"

I tell them the road intersects with the highway that

leads to the entrance to the park. "But we can't go that way. They'll know we climbed to the rim, and . . ."

"Yeah," Glinda says, nodding slowly. "And they'll figure out why."

"So, why did your dad bring you here?" X looks at me. "He must've had a reason for bringing you here."

"To see the Lighthouse. There's a good view of it over there." I point toward the rim where Dad took me the first day. "I, uh, I think he climbed down to it from up here, but we can't tell. Warden Winnie would probably report him. He'd lose his job and might not get hired at other places."

"Man-oh-man," Bobby Ray mumbles. "We're in a real pickle."

"Well, we have to do something," Glinda says. "And soon. Search parties are prob'ly looking for us already. They all have those walkie-talkies."

"We go down." I start walking through the brush toward the rim. "We climb down to the Lighthouse. It's the only thing that makes sense. We told our folks that's where we were going, so it's the logical place to be."

"Down?" Bobby Ray says. "But that's crazy. We just got *up*."

"No, she's right," Glinda says, trotting after me.

"Just to the pedestal at the bottom of the Lighthouse," X says, lifting Héctor onto his back. "That's as far as we need to go."

"But that's off trail." I look over my shoulder at X. "And we're not supposed to leave the trail."

"But it would be the safest place, because the Lighthouse would've shielded us from the wind and rain. It would make sense to them."

"Especially since Héctor was hurt," Bobbie Ray says.

"Yeah, but how'd Héctor get hurt?" Glinda says. "I mean, he couldn't have gotten hurt like that falling *on* the trail. So they'll know we left the trail."

"'Cause I had to go," Héctor says. "I tell them I went to pee and fell down." He leans down so he can look at his brother. "And it's not a lie, huh, X? 'Cause I found them when I had to go pee that day."

"Well, not a bad lie," X says.

"A slap on the wrist," Bobby Ray says. "That's all they'll do, give us a slap on the wrist. You see it all the time on those cop shows."

"There it is." Stopping at the rim, I look at the Lighthouse. It looks huge after the rainstorm. Taller, somehow, and redder in the sunrise. "Down we go."

The climb down goes fast. The rain scoured the trail clear of loose rock, so the footing is better. When we reach the pedestal, we take out our binoculars.

"See anyone?" My hands are shaking so badly, I can't focus my glasses.

"No," X says, "but I hear engines. ATVs, probably. They'd be faster than hiking in."

"A pact . . ." Bobby Ray holds out a hand, palm down. "We keep everyone's secrets and apologize like crazy. Our folks will be so happy to see us, they won't stay mad for long."

We each lay a hand on top of his.

"Ranger Burns, too?' Héctor says. "You think she won't stay mad, either?"

"Don't know about her." Bobby Ray shrugs. "The warden's kind of unpredictable."

“I don’t care.” Glinda grins. “This has been the best summer ever.”

“Look.” Removing his shirt, X waves it like a flag. “We’re being rescued.”

Below, I see Dad scaling the slope like a mountain goat.

CHAPTER THIRTY-SEVEN

"I take full responsibility," Dad tells Ranger Burns. "Had other things on my mind and didn't pay attention to the weather."

We rode back to the trailhead in ATVs. Everyone was there waiting for us. Mr. García. Glinda's and Bobby Ray's parents. Ranger Burns. They all look as wrecked as we do.

"Guess it could've been a lot worse," Ranger Burns says, examining our bruises and cuts. "Everyone okay?"

We nod like bobblehead dolls on car dashboards.

"Good job with Héctor's leg," she says, looking at Bobby Ray. "Can't be too prepared."

"My mom taught me," he says.

"I'm an emergency room nurse." Mrs. Jones wraps an arm around Bobby Ray's shoulder. She's a thin woman with scrubbed-looking skin.

Ranger Burns looks at Héctor again. "How'd you say you got that?"

"I had to go pee."

"You okay, *m'ijo*?" Mr. García examines Héctor's bandage.

"*Sí*, Papá. It's just a scratch."

"We're still guides, aren't we?" I look at Ranger Burns. "You're still going to let us be guides, aren't you?"

"I don't know. . . ." She hesitates. "A guide's supposed to a set a good example."

Dad says, "They made some good decisions, Winnie. In an unpredictable situation."

"Yes, I suppose they did." She looks at us. "All right. Take today to rest up, come in Tuesday morning. If nothing else, you learned a good lesson."

We turn into bobbleheads again.

"I keep Héctor with me a few days," Mr. García says. "Until he is better."

Everyone separates for the drive back.

"Dad . . ." I slide into the truck. "You didn't call Mom, did you?"

"Thought about it," he says, squeezing my hand. "But decided not to. As cautious as you are, didn't figure you'd do anything too foolhardy."

I just smile.

CHAPTER THIRTY-EIGHT

Ranger Burns is waiting for us on Tuesday morning. Her eyes are dark marbles beneath the brim of her hat. Her cheeks spotted with bright color.

"Conference room—now."

"*Uh-oh,*" Glinda whispers.

"Remember our pact," Bobby Ray says. "Don't cave."

We sit at the conference table, watching Ranger Burns pace up and down.

"Help me out here." She eyes us as she paces. "Why was it you needed to hike the Lighthouse Trail?" She stops walking to look at me. "Believe that was your idea, wasn't it, Cassandra?"

When an adult uses your proper name, you know you're in trouble.

Except when Dad says it . . .

"I'm confused," I mumble. "Do I need to raise my hand if you call me by name?"

"No," she snaps. "But as I recall, it was because it was

the park's most famous landmark, and you were the only one who hadn't gotten to see it. That sound about right?"

"Yeah, but I've seen it now. So if you want to put me back on the two-milers, it's okay."

"So you're saying your *curiosity* has been satisfied?" She resumes her pacing.

"Totally."

"Well . . ." She stops in front of me again. "Mine hasn't. You see, something most *curious* happened on Sunday . . . the same day you all went hiking." She stops to look around the table. "Those missing Plano points turned up—right after that storm. How do you suppose that happened?"

X's hand inches up. "Maybe the wind blew sand over them. Probably there all the time and just got covered up."

"Yeah." I swallow over the lump in my throat. "And the rain uncovered them. It was really coming down."

"Makes sense to me," Glinda says.

"Yup," Bobby Ray says, nodding all three chins. "Totally."

"*That's* what you think?" Ranger Burns's eyebrows knit together. "Well, it's a plausible theory, I suppose . . . except archaeologists map everything on grids *and* protect finds in bad weather to ensure nothing's damaged. They swear those points just reappeared like . . . *magic*."

She resumes pacing, shaking her head. "*Magic* . . . You know who performs magic?"

"Magicians?" I giggle. The others do, too.

Spinning around, Ranger Burns locks her eyes on me. "Right—*sorcerers*. Magicians who influence fate . . . the outcome of things."

She walks to where I'm sitting and looks down at me. "You believe in magic, Cassandra?"

"Um . . ." I lift my shoulders, let them drop. "Is there a right answer to that question?"

"*Here's* the right answer," she sputters. "I—do—not—believe—in—magic. I don't know why or how, but I think whoever masterminded the return of those points is in this room."

"I do," Bobby Ray says quickly. "I believe in magic, 'cause sometimes magical things happen." He takes hold of Glinda's hand. "Like, when a fat boy gets a cute girlfriend and he doesn't even have to do her homework 'cause she's smart, too."

Glinda blushes clear to the tips of her pixie cut. X and I grin at each other.

Ranger Burns's mouth drops open. "Oh, for pity's sake . . ." Sighing, she waves her hand toward the door. "Get out of here, just . . . get out. You have students waiting."

We march out of the room, single file.

"And keep your noses clean," she yells from the doorway. "No shenanigans!"

We give her mock salutes.

"And Cassie," she yells.

"Yes, ma'am?" I turn slowly, hoping she hasn't changed her mind.

"Tell your dad to get his butt in here tomorrow morning before he starts work. I'll have the papers ready for him to sign."

"Uh, yes, ma'am." I watch her stalk away.

Papers?

CHAPTER THIRTY-NINE

"What do you think, Ti?" I've taken him for a walk on his leash to the boulder field in back of the Winnebago. "Where do you think Dad's next job is? Prob'ly a long way off, huh?"

Ti's ears swivel toward the Winnebago. Turning, I see Dad walking toward us.

"What are you doing out here?" he calls.

"This is one of Ti's favorite spots," I say.

"It is pretty." Climbing up the boulders, he sits down with us and looks toward the cliffs, which the sunset is coloring russet and red. "Too bad he can't see it."

"Oh, I describe it to him."

"You talk to him?"

"Sure. About all kinds of things. The stars . . . the campfires . . . horned lizards. All kinds of things."

Dad just smiles.

"Um, Dad. Warden Winnie told me to give you a message."

"*Warden* Winnie?"

"That's the nickname we gave her—*I* gave her." I grin at him. "She can be pretty bossy."

He shakes his head slightly. "You don't like her much, do you?"

"No. Yes. I mean, I didn't at first, but now . . ."

The hint of a grin shows. "What'd she say?"

"For you to get your butt to the office before you start work tomorrow"—I look at him—"so you can sign the papers."

"I see." He pauses to scratch Ti on the head. "She tell you what kind of papers?"

"No. But you went to town on Sunday to send an e-mail, so I figure the papers are about a new job somewhere."

He nods slowly. "How do you feel about moving away?"

I set Ti on the boulder between us. "I don't know. Okay, I guess. But I'll miss the U-Turns."

"U-Turns?"

"Oh, that's what we call our gang. You know, the kids I've been doing stuff with."

"A gang . . . you joined a gang."

"Well, we call it a society. Bobby Ray wanted to call us a bunch, but we voted him down because we didn't want to sound like grapes."

"A horse by any other name," he says, laughing.

"Yeah," I say, grinning. "But tattoos are off-limits."

"Good. Peach hair is about as much as I can handle."

"Peach? In case you haven't noticed, the sun has bleached the tips to corn husks." I pick up a pebble and flip it away. "So before we leave, I'd like to get a haircut. Time to go back to mousy brown."

"You mean, back to the real you," Dad says. "There's

a barber shop on the square. Go there myself. Barber's pretty good, and you don't need to make an appointment. Walk-ins are welcome."

"Barber shop? Geez, Dad. I might as well have Pearl cut it."

"I'm sure she'd be glad to accommodate you."

"No, thanks. I'll find out where Glinda got hers cut."

His face turns serious. "The papers I'm signing tomorrow *are* about a new job, Cassie. Two new jobs, as a matter of fact."

"Two jobs? Are the Garcías going with us after all?" My heart pounds against my ribs.

"Nope, both jobs are for me. Winnie's been on my back all summer to go to work for her as property manager."

So *that's* why she's been watching him so close. . . .

"I'll be hiring contractors to do the work rather than doing it myself," he says.

"Contractors . . . You mean, like Mr. García?"

"Exactly," he says, smiling.

"But wait, what about your dream? You wanted to see the wider world, be your own boss—" I catch my breath. "It's because of me, isn't it? You're staying put because of me." Tears well up in my eyes.

"I wasn't finished," he says. "She's offered me flexible hours so I can complete park ranger training, too."

"Ranger? You're going to be a park ranger?"

"Yep. I'll be assigned here a year or two, and then I can apply for reassignment to other parks. And if you think about it, rangers are pretty much their own boss. Seemed like a good idea all the way around." He gives my head a rub. "Best of all, I get to spend my off time with you."

"But the e-mail, what about the e-mail?"

"Needed to cancel a job I bid on, that's all."

"Two jobs . . . Can you still homeschool me?"

"I've been thinking about that," he says. "How would you feel about attending the school in town? You could ride the bus with X and Héctor."

"Ohmigosh."

"What is it?"

"Glinda and Bobby Ray go to that school. That'd be great. On my first day of school, I'll already have friends."

"So . . ." He wraps an arm around my shoulders. "You okay with everything?"

"Are you kidding? *Totally* okay."

Yay, me.

CASSANDRA'S ~~CASSIE'S DETECTIVE~~ JOURNAL

No suspicious behavior or clues to report. Just a few things I learned this summer about being a detective:

1. Sometimes "clues" are just ordinary things that we misinterpret.
2. Suspicions are mostly fears we let freak us out if we let our imagination run wild.

<u>Other things I learned</u>

1. Sometimes the blind can see better than those with eyesight.
2. Blisters heal and make you tough.
3. It's okay to break the rules . . . sometimes.
4. You can find magic in the most unexpected places.
5. Don't rush to judge. Things aren't always what they seem.
6. To add spice to life, don't be afraid to change up the recipe.

ABOUT THE AUTHOR

Seeking Cassandra evolved naturally for Lutricia Clifton, as she lived in the Texas Panhandle from the third grade through junior college. Palo Duro Canyon was a favorite retreat for her family. They spent many weekends there, hiking, exploring and picnicking.

After completing a BA and an MA in English at Colorado State University, Clifton worked in business and journalism. She now lives in northern Illinois with a brown tabby named Mary Jane and focuses on spending quality time with family and writing fiction.

Clifton has published two other middle-grade novels with Holiday House: *Freaky Fast Frankie Joe* and *Immortal Max*.